The California Experiment

Russell Fine

Russell Fine
11/26/19

Other Novels
By
Russell Fine

Future World History I 2024-2120
Future World History II 2120-2136
Future World History III - The Final Chapter
Frank Carver Mysteries
Frank Carver Mysteries - Volume 2

Dedication

This book is dedicated to all those people who helped make this book a reality:

First, I want to thank my wife, Sherry, who provided valuable assistance all through this entire project by acting as a sounding board for my ideas regarding the plot, correcting my frequent typing errors, and editing and formatting the final version of the book.

My son, Randy, who gave me some helpful ideas for the plot and also provided assistance in editing.

My friends, and neighbors, Suzanne Horsfall and Cheryl Adamkiewicz who thoroughly read the manuscript, and provided assistance by correcting both plot and keying errors.

Finally, I also want to thank my friends and fellow authors, Sharon Higa and BJ Gillum for providing valuable assistance with the final editing.

Preface

Adam Peterson was one of the richest and most powerful men in the United States, but because he craved anonymity, he was not well known outside his circle of close associates. He lived in a modest home in Palo Alto and drove his five-year-old Ford to his office in San Jose every day. Adam was forty-three years old, and spent most of the last twenty years building his business empire. He was six feet tall, balding, and at least twenty pounds overweight. He felt his personal appearance was unimportant, so he always wore jeans and polo shirts to work. When he wasn't busy, which was rare, he thought about his personal life and realized he never spent much time building relationships. He never married, and never had a serious relationship with a woman.

When he was twenty, he started a software company that produced games for handheld devices. But his games were different. They were fun to play and never became so difficult that they became frustrating. He charged a dollar a month for access to all of his games. After six months, he had over a million subscribers, and by the end of his third year that number had risen to more than twenty million. Then he convinced two of the major cell phone service providers to include his games on all their cell phones. He paid them a dime for each dollar he received from their users, and just a year later, Peterson Gaming was pulling in almost a hundred million dollars a month. It was the largest privately held company in the United States.

Adam began buying other companies, including a controlling interest in several smaller cell phone providers. Ten years after he started his company, he owned or controlled more than thirty companies with combined annual sales of more than fifteen billion dollars.

He dreamed about using his wealth to buy political influence, and when he had the money, that's exactly what he did. Because he wanted to remain anonymous, he employed a group of operatives to spread his wealth around, never contacting any politicians directly. He discovered it was fairly easy to influence politicians with cash, and at the age of thirty-seven, he had the ability to control the California legislature. He decided to extend his reach to the federal government as well. It was a little more expensive to influence members of the House and Senate, but not substantially so.

Now he had achieved his dream. But he still wasn't happy. He had always been liberal, and despite the fact that capitalism allowed him to realize his dream, he believed socialism was a superior form of government. His party lost the 2020 election and the republicans regained control of the house. In 2022, the democrats regained many of the seats they lost in 2020, but the republicans had maintained a slim majority. He was sure the country was turning more liberal, and was positive with sufficient financial backing, a socialist could win in 2024.

He used his influence to get Cathy Mitchell, the socialist senator recently elected in a special election in Oregon, the nomination for president from the Democratic party for the 2024 election. He spent more than three hundred million dollars to promote her to the American electorate, but she lost in a landslide. She only won five states; California, New York, Illinois, Oregon, and Washington. To make matters even worse, the Democrats lost all of their gains from the previous election. In the House, the Republicans now held a forty-seat majority, and controlled sixty-eight seats in the Senate.

The election was ten days earlier and he had been thinking about what action he could take that would help the situation. He decided there was only one possible course of action. He called his assistant, Ellen Miller, and told her to set up a meeting with all of his political operatives within the next forty-eight hours. The meeting was scheduled for Monday, November 18 at 10:00 AM.

He arrived at the meeting room at precisely 10:00 o'clock, walked in, and received a standing ovation from his employees. He smiled and walked to the podium in the front of the room.

"Good morning. To get right to the point I, like all of you, am very upset about the election results. I've been thinking about what course of action we could possibly take that would help with our situation. I realized late last week that there is only one thing we can do. That is to secede from the United States. We will become our own country, with our own laws, and more importantly, our own government. California's economy is the fifth largest in the world. There's no reason we couldn't make it on our own."

Adam paused to wait for a reaction. For a few seconds everyone was silent. Then someone stood and began to applaud. Moments later everyone in the meeting room was standing and applauding as well.

Adam smiled and nodded indicating for them to sit. When the room became quiet, he continued. "Obviously we must plan this very carefully. The United States government is not going to sit idly by when they find out what we plan to do. We must be prepared to fight for what we believe in. We don't have an army, but we do have the ability to put an economic stranglehold on the United States Government. I want each of you to contact the politicians you work with and ask them how they feel about the idea. Feel free to threaten them if necessary. While you are working on that, I will put together an economic plan to bring those assholes in DC to their knees."

Everyone stood up and began to applaud again. Adam smiled, then left the podium and walked out of the room.

Russell Fine

I
The Plan

After the meeting, Adam went back to his office. As he passed Ellen's desk, he asked her to come with him. She wasn't at the meeting, but she knew what Adam wanted to do. She told him bluntly that his plan would never work, but she would help him anyway.

Ellen joined Peterson Gaming shortly after Adam formed the company. She was twenty-three at the time and had just graduated from U.C. Davis with a degree in computer engineering. She started her career as a programmer, but Adam quickly realized she had some great ideas for marketing. So, when he formed a marketing department, he put Ellen in charge.

Two years later, Adam promoted her and she became Vice-President, and his assistant. That was almost fifteen years ago, and he knew he needed her. She was a voice of reason and had the ability to calm him down when he lost his temper, which was a fairly frequent occurrence.

Ellen walked in and said dryly, "I'm sure they were all thrilled with your idea."

"Yes, it appeared that way. Now, if I could only convince you that it's a good idea, I would be a happy man."

"Sorry to burst your bubble; you know how I feel about it."

"Yes, I do. Anyway, I want you to compile a list of California based companies that have large federal contracts to supply goods and services. I'm specifically interested in companies that are the sole supplier of the products they sell."

"Are you going to ask them to stop selling to the feds?"

"No, I want them to continue to supply their products, but at substantially increased prices. Then we'll take the increased profits from them to fund our new country."

"What will you do if they refuse?"

Adam smiled and said, "That's easy. We take control of the company. I'll make that abundantly clear when I meet with them."

"So, you're going to give up your precious anonymity?"

"I have no choice. How long do you think it will take to compile the list?"

"Give me a week."

"Okay, but not a day longer."

Ellen wanted to say, "Do it yourself. I quit!", but instead she said, "Yes, sir."

During the next few days, all of his political operatives called to give him a report about how things went with the legislators. Almost all liked the idea, but the general consensus was that they wanted to have a detailed plan before they would consider supporting it publicly.

Ellen had the list completed right on time. It was sitting on Adam's desk when he arrived at his office on Monday, November 25th. He quickly read through the list. There were seventy-three companies listed. Most of them supplied parts for the military. The companies varied in size from as few as twenty-five employees to an electronics company with over thirty thousand employees.

Next, he had to figure out how to approach them. He decided to start with the smaller companies. He selected Becker Aerospace for his first contact. The company had fifty-seven employees. They manufactured several key components for jet fighters used by all of the branches of the military.

He spent the next several hours researching the company. Their sales in 2023 were almost two hundred fifty million dollars, and all of their sales were to the federal government. His research revealed that the sole owner of the company was Harold Becker. He graduated from UCLA with a degree in mechanical engineering. After he graduated, he joined the Air Force. During his four-year stint in the Air Force, he spent his time managing aircraft maintenance people. When he left the Air Force, he borrowed money to start Becker Aerospace. Somehow, Harold Becker managed to acquire the rights to the products they were currently manufacturing, and his company is the sole supplier of those aircraft components.

Adam began to have second thoughts about contacting Becker Aerospace because he was concerned Harold Becker might be a conservative. However, he decided that if he could convince Becker to support secession, he could probably convince anyone.

He called Becker Aerospace. When the receptionist answered the phone, he asked to speak with Harold Becker. The receptionist asked who was calling, and then she put the call through. The next thing Adam heard was a man saying, "This is Harold Becker. How can I assist you, Mr. Peterson?"

Adam replied, "Thank you for taking my call, Mr. Becker. I have a matter of some urgency I would like to discuss with you in person. Could I stop by your office tomorrow morning?"

"I believe you are the owner of Peterson Gaming. Is that correct?"

"Yes, it is. However, this matter has nothing to do with my company. I need your help with something that I don't feel comfortable discussing over the phone."

"Okay, how about 10 o'clock?"

"That will be perfect. I'll see you tomorrow."

Peterson Gaming owned a small business jet and Adam was a licensed pilot. He arrived at the San Jose Airport few minutes after six, filed a flight plan to go the Burbank Airport, and left shortly before seven. After landing, he rented a car and drove to Becker Aerospace. He was standing at the receptionist's desk at five minutes to ten. He gave the woman at the desk his card and said he had an appointment with Mr. Becker.

Adam was wearing a blue business suit instead of his usual attire. He was pleased when, a few minutes later, a tall, thin man, dressed in jeans and a polo shirt, walked into the reception area. He smiled at Adam and said, "Good morning, Mr. Peterson. I'm Harold Becker. Please come in."

Adam stood, shook hands with Harold and said, "I'm pleased to meet you. Thank you for taking the time to meet with me."

"I must tell you that I'm really curious why you wanted to meet with me. I don't believe we have common interests."

"I'll explain everything. Can we meet somewhere private?"

"Sure, the conference room is empty. Would you like some coffee?"

"No, thank you."

They walked to the conference room and sat on opposite sides of the table. Then Adam put his briefcase on the table and removed a device that looked like a cell phone. He turned it on, waved it around a little, and put it back into his briefcase. Harold smiled and said, "There's no reason to check for bugs."

"Mr. Becker, I need your assurance that the information I'm about to discuss with you will remain confidential."

"You have it. So, tell me, why are you here?"

"I represent a group of people who were devastated with the results of the election. We believe some action must be taken in order to be sure we maintain our goals for California."

"I'm sorry to inform you that I'm not the least bit upset with the results of the election."

"You are, of course, entitled to your opinion. However, because your company is based in California, you will be affected by the actions we are about to take. We plan to secede from the United States and form our own country."

Harold stared at Adam for several seconds before saying, "You're serious, aren't you?"

"Yes, I'm absolutely serious. This is going to happen. The legislature will vote on the plan within the next month."

Again, Harold paused before he replied, "Aside from the fact that I think that's a really awful idea, do you really believe the United States government is going to let you do that?"

"Mr. Becker, your company is one of many that are the sole supplier for items the United States government needs. If they try to stop us, they will suddenly find themselves unable to purchase the goods and services they need. Additionally, we will not allow goods destined for the United States that arrive at our ports to move through our new country. We believe those two factors alone are sufficient to keep the United States military at bay. Of course, we'll need a lot of money to make this plan a success, and the only way we can do that is to get it from the United States. So, we're going to ask all of the companies based in California to raise their prices substantially, and send the excess profit to the California treasury. That includes your company, Mr. Becker."

"And if I refuse?"

"Then the California government will simply nationalize your company."

"So, you plan to model our new country after Nazi Germany?"

"No, but I won't allow anyone to stand in the way of our ultimate success. If you do as we ask, you will continue to operate Becker Aerospace as you see fit."

"Until California makes additional demands. Then the threats will start again. Don't you think you should at least allow people the opportunity to vote for or against secession? After all, they did that in England when they left the EU."

"We don't believe that's necessary. The residents of California elected people to represent them in the legislature, and they have confidence in their ability to govern."

"Mr. Peterson, I gave you my promise that I won't discuss this with anyone, and I will abide by that. However, you have worn out your welcome. Please leave."

"Okay, I'm leaving. But rest assured, we'll be speaking again."

Adam closed his brief case, stood up, and left the conference room. The meeting went exactly as he suspected it would. He was positive that when the time came, Becker would acquiesce to the California government's demands.

Over the next few days, Adam met with several more companies based in the bay area. In every case, the companies agreed to provide whatever assistance was needed to make the secession a reality.

Adam set up another meeting with his political operatives. The meeting was held in a large conference room at a nearby hotel. When everyone was seated, he asked each of them to give a report. The general consensus was that the legislature would do whatever Adam felt was needed. Then he told them about his meetings with the California based companies. So far, everything was moving along smoothly. Then he told them he wanted checkpoints built at every place a major highway crosses the California border.

Someone asked, "Won't that give away our plan?"

Adam replied, 'There's nothing to give away. I guarantee you; the President is already aware of our plans. I'm sure that if I can buy legislators, the feds can buy them too. But that cannot deter us from our goal. They won't do anything until we make our secession public, so we must be prepared to act decisively. The purpose of the checkpoints is to prevent goods from being shipped out of California by truck without the payment of fees. We will also be checking ships and planes before they will be allowed to leave. Additionally, any banking transaction that exceeds one hundred thousand dollars will have to be approved by a banking regulator."

"Will we allow people to leave?"

Adam answered, "Of course, but we will limit what they can take with them."

"So, if someone sells their house, they won't be able to leave the state with the proceeds from the sale. Is that right?"

"Exactly. Real estate transactions for people leaving California will be heavily taxed. The same thing will apply to the sale of businesses. The whole idea is that money generated in California stays in California."

"Don't you think the United States will reciprocate and prevent us from buying the things we need from them?"

"That's a definite possibility. So, if we need something we don't make here, we'll purchase it from countries other than the United States. However, I believe we can be largely self-sufficient. We can grow our own food, supply our own energy, and manufacturer the things our people need. Initially there'll probably be some be some shortages, but I feel confident they will be short term. Remember, the United States does not manufacture nearly what they used to. They import far more than they make."

"Do you plan on us having our own currency?"

"No, we'll continue to use the United States dollar. If they give us a hard time, we'll switch to the Chinese yuan. It's as widely accepted as the United States dollar."

Adam paused for a few moments and then continued. "These laws I just spoke about, and much more, will be sent to each of you in the next ten days. I want you to make sure they're submitted to the legislature and put into the proper format so they can be voted on immediately after secession. Also, if your contacts don't feel comfortable with this move, feel free to apply whatever pressure is necessary to insure these measures pass."

Someone asked, "After secession, who will be in charge? Will Governor Nelson assume control of our country?"

"There will be a special election within sixty days after secession to elect a president and vice-president. Governor Nelson will become interim president and retain that position until the results of the election can be determined."

"Are you going to run for president?"

"I haven't made that decision yet. If any of you have any questions or problems, please contact me. The next few months are going to both hectic and very exciting. I'm sure there will be some roadblocks along the way, so it's imperative that I'm informed about them as soon as possible. Thank you all for coming. This meeting is adjourned"

Russell Fine

II

The Oval Office
April 7, 2025

President Nancy Haskell was sitting on the sofa. Her chief of staff, Roy Stuart, sat directly across from her. He said, "It would appear the California legislature will have the secession vote within thirty days and it will pass easily. I know we've discussed this before, but I feel strongly we must take some action to prevent that from happening."

"I know how you feel, but the only overt action we could take to prevent secession would involve the use of the military. I don't want to start a civil war, or at least not one that has us shooting at each other. I believe the best approach would be to have an economic war. We already know what actions they're going to take, so we have to counter them with actions of our own."

"I understand, but I think we have to make it so painful for them, no other state will ever try it. I think that may involve more than economics."

"Perhaps, but we will have to wait to see what effect our economic sanctions have. Did you get any response to your request to find additional vendors for all of the single source items used by the military?"

"Yes, they all thought it was a good idea, and agreed to do that as quickly as possible. I didn't tell them about California possibly seceding. I just told them it wasn't a good idea to have a single supplier for anything they purchase."

"Did you contact the shipping companies and request they reroute their ships to ports in Oregon and Washington?"

"Yes, but there's a problem. Most of those shipments contain products for California. To do what you asked would be very expensive for them. They want us to pay for any additional expenses they incur as a result of our request. I'm sure you've thought about this already; what happens if Oregon or Washington follow California and secede too?"

"They may be thinking about it, but I'm positive they won't take any action until they see how we handle the California situation.

13

Find out what the shipping companies think it will cost to reroute their ships."

"Okay. By the way, I was just informed that construction of the border checkpoints will begin next week. Once that happens, everyone with half a brain will realize what's going on."

"Yeah, I'm sure you're right. I think one other action we may have to take would involve support for groups within California that are less than pleased with the idea of becoming an independent country. We should help incite incidents of insurrection and see how they handle it. Perhaps some former military personnel would like to handle that for us. Could you look into that as well?"

"That's a great idea," Roy said with a big smile on his face. "I should have thought of that before. I have some contacts who may be able to help us. I'll get on it right away."

"Good, please keep me informed."

"Of course."

III
Sacramento, California
April 24, 2025

The Governor of California, Gary Nelson, was sitting at his desk. In front of him were TV cameras from every major television network. At precisely 7:00 o'clock he began to speak.

"Good evening. Tomorrow the California legislature will vote on the most important piece of legislation in our state's history. As you are all aware, our values and ideals are not the same as those of the federal government. In fact, there are very few issues where we are in agreement. It was my hope, and yours, that the last election would have resolved the problem. However, it only served to make the situation worse. Our differences are irreconcilable, and so our only choice is to sever our relationship with the United States.

"Tomorrow, the legislature will vote to determine if we remain part of the United States, or we become an independent country. However, I can tell you now that by this time tomorrow we will no longer be the State of California, we will, instead, be the country of California.

"We have been planning this action for months, and although we have tried to make the transition as smooth as possible, we are certain there will be some problems. We will do our best to minimize the effect these problems have on our citizens, but we ask for your patience during the next several months.

"First, I want you to be aware that I will assume the position as president on a temporary basis. There will be an election held within sixty days to elect a president who will serve a four-year term.

"Starting a new country is a daunting task. We must make sure California is solvent, and remains that way. In order to do that, the legislature will be passing new laws and regulations that will increase our revenues. A list of these measures will be published after the vote tomorrow. But I can assure you, your tax burden will not increase. The money you previously paid to the federal government will now be paid to the country of California.

"The United States government owns buildings and vacant land in California. Those holdings will all be annexed by California.

We will give them ninety days to vacate all their properties, including military bases. Many of these properties will be used to house the influx of immigrants we are expecting.

"Our goal is to have an open society. To that end, the walls that have been built on our southern border will be demolished, and our border with Mexico will be open. Many of you are probably aware that we have built border checkpoints along all major highways that connect California with the United States. Those checkpoints are not to keep people out of California. They were built to collect fees from trucks transporting goods out of our country. We will be building similar checkpoints on rail lines. We believe these fees will become a major source of revenue for us.

"Many of you have requested a single payer health system. To make that happen, all private health facilities will be nationalized, and all medical personnel will become California employees. You will be able to go to any doctor, or any hospital, and receive free medical care.

"We will also be taking control of all federally chartered banks. We will relinquish that control when they agree to abide by new banking rules that have been drawn up by the legislature. Additionally, we will be nationalizing all utility companies in California. Your electric, water, sewage, and natural gas bills will now be generated by the government. We are doing this to make sure you pay a fair price for the services you use.

"Our colleges and universities will also be tuition free for our residents. None of our citizens will graduate from college with debt that will take them decades to pay.

"This is only the beginning. California is destined to become a utopia. We will be the envy of the rest of the world, and all of you will be a part of it.

"Thank you. I will speak to you again soon."

IV
The Oval Office
April 25, 2025

Roy Stuart walked into the President Haskell's office and said, "Good morning, Madam President. I assume you saw Nelson's speech last night. Is your response ready?"

"Yes, I've called a press conference for two o'clock. There was nothing unexpected in the speech. We've already begun drawing down our military presence in California. My concern is the number of people who will be out of a job as a result of this ridiculous move. I assume congress is going to vote today on the Federal Employee Relief Act?"

"Yes, the House will vote on it this morning, and the Senate will vote on it this afternoon. It will be on your desk before six o'clock."

"Good, we need to let them know we will help them through this mess. Have we resolved the issue of single source military components?"

"Yes, every contractor based in California sent us a letter terminating our existing contracts indicating that prices for the products they were making for us would increase by two hundred percent. We replied to everyone and told them we have contracted with another supplier. They were not pleased, to say the least. As a result, many of these companies will go out of business. One of those companies is owned by someone I worked with when I was in the Air Force. His name is Harold Becker. He called me yesterday and told me he was going to be forced to close his business. He was not concerned for himself. He lives alone. His wife died a few years ago and he never had any children. But he is worried about his employees. He also indicated that he would be willing to help us if we decide to take any covert action against the California government."

"That could be very useful. Let's get some people working on this. I don't want anybody hurt, but I want any action we take to cost California a lot of money."

Roy smiled and said, "Of course. However, I want to do this on my own. I don't want you directly involved. I want you to be able to deny any knowledge of the actions we take."

"I appreciate that. Also, I've been thinking, as we vacate the buildings and military bases, I want every piece of useful equipment removed. I want to leave them just the bare structures."

"That seems reasonable, and I'm sure it will be unexpected. Anything else?"

"Yes, I want armed guards at all military bases and federal office buildings. I don't want anybody from the California government on those premises before we're ready to vacate them."

"That's an excellent idea. I'm sure we can arrange that within a day or two."

"Then, let's meet again in two days."

V
The White House Briefing Room
April 25, 2025

After a brief introduction by her press secretary, Mark Dickenson, President Haskell walked up to the podium and began to speak. "Thank you all for coming. Please understand that I will not be taking any questions during this briefing. However, I believe that your questions will be answered by my prepared statement.

"Yesterday, the State of California made the decision to withdraw from our union and become an independent country. I realize we have very little in common with California at this time, but becoming an independent country is an act of total incompetence. However, the only way to prevent them from seceding would be use of military force. I don't wish to have a second civil war, and I want to avoid casualties on both sides. So, no military action will be taken at this time. We have been aware of this possibility for several months, and are prepared to take actions that will isolate California economically.

"First, we have found new suppliers for items we previously purchased from companies located in California. We took this action because they cancelled the contracts they had with us, and attempted to increase their prices substantially. Also, they're planning on charging shipping companies for shipping goods out of California. Those charges would be passed on to our consumers, and could hurt our economy. To minimize the effect of these fees, all goods that were to arrive at California ports destined for other locations will be routed to ports in Oregon and Washington. Obviously, if consumers wish to purchase goods made in California, they are welcome to do so. We will not impose tariffs on California products, unless they impose them on products we manufacture.

"They have ordered us to vacate all federal buildings and military bases. We will do that, but we will leave nothing useful behind. Items we can't use or would be too expensive to move will be destroyed.

"We began reducing our military presence in California three months ago, and the number of current military personnel stationed there is already down by almost fifty percent.

"They have implemented a number of new laws that make it very difficult for their current residents to move out. The most onerous is a tax on real estate sales that allows the state to collect up to fifty percent of the sale price. For most people, their home is the most expensive thing they will ever buy, and many are dependent on the increased value of their homes to provide them with financial security. To counteract this, we will be offering financial incentives for people who leave California and relocate to the United States.

"There are thousands of federal employees in California, and they will probably find themselves out of work shortly. By the end of the day I will sign the Federal Employee Relief Act. This legislation will provide funds to help federal employees relocate to the United States. We will also make every effort to find jobs for these displaced workers.

"I want to make it crystal clear; we will not allow California to take advantage of us. They will have to make it on their own, or at least without any assistance from the United States. We will have another briefing in a few days, and at that time, I will take questions if you have submitted them prior to the briefing. Thank you for coming."

Several of the members of the press began shouting questions at the President, but she ignored them and left the room.

The following morning, Roy Stuart was sitting at his desk. He was reading a poll taken after President Haskell's new briefing and was please to find that she had the support of seventy-two percent of the people questioned. That was particularly good news since the poll was taken by the New York Times. His phone rang and when he answered it his secretary said that Harold Becker wanted to speak with him. He told her to put the call through.

"Good morning, Mr. Becker, how are things going?"

"Not great, Becker Aerospace is now out of business. Although the factory is still open and I'm paying my employees. I wanted you to know that all of my employees are ex-military and every one of them wants to help bring down the California government."

"I don't think we should be having this discussion on an open line."

"We're not. I have a friend who works at the FBI office in LA. I'm using his phone which is a secure line."

"Good, have you given any thought regarding my request for covert action?"

"It has been on my mind constantly. I've been discussing this with my employees and we've picked out more than a dozen potential targets, but we need something from you."

"What would that be?"

"Explosives. I have two former Army Rangers who have been thoroughly trained on the use of explosives, but we have no way to acquire what we need."

"I can take care of that. I'm glad you're keeping the factory open. If you need any financial assistance, let me know. We'll pay you and your employees. Send me a list of what you need and I'll have it delivered from one of the local Army bases."

"I think we're being watched, so don't send an Army vehicle. I don't want to raise any suspicions. Thank you for offering to pay me and my people, but it really isn't necessary. I have enough money to continue to pay them for several months. I hope this will all be over by then."

"It's a nice thought, but I am fairly sure it will take longer than that. I heard a rumor that they have substantial cash reserves, possibly as much as three hundred billion dollars. It could be enough to keep them going for a year or two."

"Where would they get that much money?"

"My guess is the Chinese. But I wouldn't put too much faith in the rumor. China will want something in exchange for that much money, and it won't be anything small. I'm sure you would know about it before it happens."

Harold was silent for several seconds while he thought about the situation. Finally, he said, "Still, that could be really bad news. If the Chinese have a financial stake in California and the government collapses, is there a possibility they will take over?"

"I suppose so. I've been worried about that too. But I don't think it's anything to be concerned about now."

"To be honest, I'm not positive the Chinese would be any worse than the gang of morons currently running California."

"Yeah, you may be right. Anyway, send me that list and call me in a few days. I'll let you know when the materials will arrive."

"I'll e-mail it to you shortly."

Roy ended the conversation. He hadn't thought seriously about the possibility that China could take over California, but now he couldn't get it out of his mind. They would need a plan to deal with that situation in the unlikely event it actually happened.

Roy received the list of materials Harold wanted two hours later. He read it and decided it was reasonable, so he forwarded the information to his contact at the Pentagon. A few minutes later he received a short message that said, "Materials requested will arrive in five days."

The following morning, Roy had a meeting scheduled with President Haskell. When he walked into her office, it was obvious she wasn't happy. He asked, "What's wrong?"

"As you know I'm trying to avoid armed conflict, but those idiots in California may force us into it. I received a message that stated, "No goods may travel out of California without the payment of fees based on the value of the items." I have no intention of paying them a dime. Any suggestions?"

"Yeah, we already have plans to move our stuff out in truck convoys. The lead truck will be an armored personnel carrier, and it will be filled with heavily armed personnel. They will ignore the barrier and stop just on the other side of the border. Then they will simply watch as the convoy crosses the border. They will take no action unless they are provoked. My guess is, the people manning the border stations will not make a move to interfere."

"And if they do?"

"We will use the minimum amount of force required to resolve the situation."

"When is the first convoy scheduled to leave California?"

"The day after tomorrow. I'll take care of everything. I guarantee you they don't want an armed conflict, because they know they'll lose."

"Okay. Have you heard from our friend, Harold Becker?"

"Yes, I spoke to him yesterday. As it turns out he only hired ex-military people as employees. Two of them were Army Rangers. They have already selected their targets. He has requested some supplies that will be required. I forwarded the list to my contact at the Pentagon. All of the requested items will be delivered to Harold's factory in five days."

"What did he ask for?"

"Do you really want to know?"

"No, I guess not. Did he tell you what he plans to do?"

"No, like you, I really don't want to know. I'd rather be surprised."

"Roy, do you think we should establish diplomatic relations with them? They have made the request."

"Not at this time. Perhaps after their election. I have a feeling the President will not be Nelson. I think it's going to be Adam Peterson."

"Is he any better?"

"Yeah, I think he'll be easier to deal with. He's a businessman, not a politician. I know he is an avowed socialist, but he deals with situations logically, not emotionally. On a totally different subject, during my conversation with Harold I had a horrible thought. We think the Chinese are considering giving California a lot of money. I'm sure it will be a loan, not a gift. If California is unable to pay them back, they're going to want something in return. Perhaps ownership of California."

"We can't let that happen! I'll discuss this with Secretary Crenshaw. We have to take some kind of pre-emptive action to prevent it."

"I agree."

Russell Fine

VI
San Francisco

Two days after California declared its independence, the decision was made to make the San Francisco Federal Building a test case. More than a hundred personnel were dispatched from the San Joaquin Depot. First, they packed up the contents of all the file cabinets, which turned out to be minimal, since most documents were stored electronically. Then they began working on all the electronic equipment. The packed items were loaded into trailers, and when the trailers were full, they were moved back to the San Joaquin Depot. When everything useful was moved, the items left were either burned in the building's incinerator or demolished with sledge hammers. They even stripped the electrical system and removed the backup generators. As a final gesture, all the elevator cables were cut and their motors demolished. By the time they were finished, there were thirty-nine trailers loaded and waiting to be moved.

The first truck convoy to leave California left the San Joaquin Depot at 2:00 PM. The convoy consisted of thirty-nine semi's, each with a fifty-three-foot-long trailer and a lead vehicle. It was an armored personnel carrier, with twenty marines inside. Each armed with pistols and automatic weapons. The convoy went north on Highway 99, and in Sacramento began traveling east on Interstate 80. When the lead vehicle was about a half mile from the border, a police car pulled in front of it and slowed down to ten miles per hour. When they arrived at the border, the police car stopped in front of the closed gate. Two policemen got out of their car and waved at the lead vehicle to stop. The driver slowed to five miles per hour but continued to go forward. When the policemen realized the convoy was not going to stop, they got out of the way quickly. The armored personnel carrier pushed the police car through the lowered gate and continued to drive forward until it was about a hundred feet into Nevada. Then it pulled over on the right shoulder and stopped. The marines got out of the vehicle and took positions on both shoulders of the road, their weapons ready in case there was any trouble.

No one made any attempt to stop the convoy. As the last truck crossed the border, the marines got back into their vehicle and followed.

When Nelson was informed about what happened, he became enraged. He immediately sent a threating message to President Haskell indicating that next time the guards would be armed and they would take whatever action was necessary to stop the convoy.

President Haskell's response was short, and to the point. It said, "We have a substantial military force, you do not. Your threats are meaningless. We will defend ourselves if necessary, and you will not be pleased with the result."

The message made Nelson even more angry than before. However, that was nothing compared to the level of anger he felt after he toured the San Francisco Federal Building the next day. One of his assistants, who toured the building with him, told him the estimated cost to make the building usable again was at least thirty million dollars. When the President heard the comment he snarled, "Those bastards won't get away with this. It's an act of war."

VII
The California – Mexico Border

The evening of the day California declared its independence, every employee of the federal government who worked at the Mexican border was notified that effective as of midnight, they were all on a four-week paid leave of absence. As a result, the following morning there wasn't one border patrol agent on duty. By noon, more than three thousand people crossed the border into California.

Immigrant support groups had set up caravans made up of residents from Mexico, Guatemala, and Honduras. They were all waiting at the border to cross into California as soon as the border patrol agents left their posts.

By the morning of the third day of California's independence, more than fourteen thousand immigrants had crossed into California. California was completely unprepared for the onslaught. The immigrants filled up every park, bus station, train station, and some even made it to the local airports. There was no food and practically no water. The few sanitary facilities that were available quickly became overwhelmed.

To make the situation even worse, many of the immigrants were ill, and crossed the border specifically to make use of the medical facilities in California. The emergency rooms at every southern California hospital were filled beyond capacity. California residents with real emergencies were forced to wait up to twelve hours before they could be seen by medical personnel. In San Diego alone, thirty-two people died while waiting for treatment.

The number of people crossing the border decreased dramatically by the fourth day, but it was still more than five hundred per day. The local police in San Diego, Chula Vista, Calexico, and El Centro would not allow the bands of immigrants to stop in their cities, so they moved northward to Escondido, Carlsbad, and Oceanside. The government in Sacramento finally realized the severity of the situation. To resolve the problem, on the sixth day, buses were sent to the border to pick up the people as they crossed and moved them to cities all over California.

They set up shelters in virtually every high school and began moving the immigrants there. But the situation was critical, and no real solution was in sight. The only possibility was to use facilities still controlled by the United States government. So, a request to use the facilities was sent to President Haskell. The request for assistance was immediately denied, followed with the comment that California created the problem, and now they would have to deal with it.

VIII
Medical Personnel and Facilities

In the months leading up to the day California became independent, Nelson realized that in order to implement their plan to provide free health care, a list was needed of all the people who held medical licenses in the state and their income. Letters were prepared for everyone in the medical field that basically stated that when California declared its independence from the United States, they would become government employees. They would receive sixty percent of their previous year's earnings, and informing them that since there was no reason to carry malpractice insurance any more, their earnings would be about the same.

The letter also stated that during the first year of being an independent county, they would not be allowed to retire, or leave California. Any attempt to do so would result in severe financial penalties, including forfeiture of all real estate holdings and the freezing of all financial assets. This applied not only to them, but their immediate family members as well.

The letters were mailed April 22, 2025, with the hope they would all be delivered before the expected disruption in mail service that was expected to occur shortly.

Letters were also sent to all California hospitals informing them that effective April 25, 2025, their hospital facilities would become the property of California, and all hospital medical personnel would become employees of California. Non-medical personnel would be immediately placed on an unpaid leave of absence until a determination could be made as to their continued usefulness to the facility.

Virtually the entire medical community in California was enraged. They all expected that when the state seceded from the United States, some changes in how medical services were dispensed would occur. However, they never expected a complete government takeover. Additionally, the doctors, nurses, and other medical personnel did not appreciate the threats implied in the letter they received.

The administrators of the hospitals expected an influx of patients after the border was opened, but they never planned for the number of people who showed up demanding medical assistance. Doctors and nurses were working twelve-hour shifts, and by the end of their shifts they were so worn out that they began to doubt their ability to treat their patients properly. Additionally, critical shortages of some medical supplies were occurring.

During those first few days, doctors and other medical personnel began to call in complaining of exhaustion and stating they would be unable to come to work. Each person who did that received a personal visit from the police, who bluntly told them to go to work, or go to jail. It was their choice. Only a few chose jail.

IX
Becker Aerospace
May 6, 2025

Harold Becker and four of his employees were in the conference room planning the night's activities. The materials Harold had requested from Roy Stuart arrived as promised, but they would not be used for their first act of insurrection.

Harold wanted to make sure nobody would blame the United States government for the attack. So, he decided not to use any of the material he received. Instead, his army rangers worked together to build four large, but unsophisticated bombs. They made the bombs with an explosive mixture of potassium chlorate and powdered aluminum surrounded by one-inch ball bearings. Detonation would be caused by a cheap digital clock. Their targets were the four largest power distribution stations in Los Angeles County. Each bomb would be thrown over the fence surrounding the facility and each would be detonated at exactly 3:00 AM. Harold estimated that at least a million people would be without power for several days, and it would cost California a million dollars to restore service.

The people who were scheduled to deliver the bombs took them home with them in their cars. Because there was a possibility of surveillance cameras monitoring their targets, each car had a printed duplicate of a license plate taped over their real plates. Additionally, each of the people would wear a full-face mask while they delivered their packages. They all left their homes at 1:00 AM and drove to the facility. The entire area was deserted at that time; no one encountered another person while they were at their targets.

At exactly 3:00 AM, all the bombs exploded. Each demolished a large portion of their target. The result was better than Harold could hope for. He did not realize that when independence was declared, the United States government cut California out of the western power grid. The overload took out almost every power facility in Southern California.

As soon as he was made aware of the situation, the President of California issued a statement condemning the act of insurrection, calling those who perpetrated it cowards and promised swift action finding the culprits.

That morning one of Harold's people hacked into the cell phone of a democratic member of the California Senate. Then he sent a message to President Nelson from the senator's phone telling him that this was only the first act of insurrection and that they would continue, until either California became a real democracy, not a socialist dictatorship, or it rejoined the United States.

X

The President's Office
Sacramento, California
May 7, 2025

President Nelson sat at his desk and yelled at Adam Peterson who was sitting across from him. "Adam, I expected some problems, but this is ridiculous. Do you think the United States is behind this attack on our power distribution system? If they are, we have to seriously consider creating our own military force. You seem remarkably calm, despite the seriousness of the attack."

"Gary, control yourself. First, from the information I received, it appears the bombs were crudely made. I'm sure if the United States was behind the attack, they would have used something more sophisticated. The damage the bombs actually created was minimal. A more powerful weapon would have demolished most of the substations, and it could have taken weeks to get them running again. We should be back up by tomorrow morning. Also, I think it was somewhat comical that they used Senator Clarke's cell phone to send you the message about the attack."

Nelson replied, angrily, "I'm not laughing. I was positive that Senator Clarke didn't send that message. However, I'm concerned that nobody thought about the possibility we would be disconnected from the power grid. This situation will occur again if any of our power generation facilities go offline. And now that these terrorists know we are vulnerable, we will very likely have more power disruptions."

"I'm sure you realize there's no way for us to create a military force. We don't have the resources, and even if we did, we would not be in a position to go to war with the United States. You're right, there will certainly be more attacks. We talked about it before, and you know there are right wing extremist groups who will feel it is their duty to hurt us anyway they can. That includes attacks like the one last night. We just have to learn to deal with these situations calmly."

Gary appeared to have calmed down somewhat. Then he said, "Speaking of resources, we never anticipated more than fifteen thousand people would cross the border that quickly after we opened it. Money is just starting to flow in from payroll taxes, but taking care of the immigrants is depleting our treasury faster than taxes can replenish it. We were hoping the United States would fund our actions, but I no longer think that's a possibility. Here, look at this."

Gary handed Adam a file, which he opened and began to read. It was a report from the treasurer which bluntly stated that at the current rate, the treasury would run out of money in six months. Adam closed the file and said, "I wasn't expecting that to happen so quickly. I thought we would have at least eighteen months to adjust our revenue streams. We're going to have to find some new revenue sources. Do you have any ideas?"

"I wish I did. I promised the people of California their taxes would not increase. Kind of like when George Bush said '*Read my lips. No new taxes.*' We know how that worked out for him. The only possibility is employer taxes."

"Before we do anything, let's have someone do a complete assessment of our finances and see how short we are to balance the budget. It may not be as bleak as it seems. Many of our revenue streams have not been fully implemented."

"Okay, I'll take care of that. By the way, did you tour the San Francisco Federal Building yet?"

"No, I was planning on doing that this week. I suppose it's pretty depressing."

"Depressing does not even begin to cover it. Sam Gilbert toured the building with me. He told me it would cost at least thirty million dollars to make the building usable again. If they do that to all their buildings, we will definitely have a problem."

"You're right, but the one bright spot was the Post Office. They turned over their buildings completely intact, and all the people who worked for the post office are now working for California, so they are still delivering mail. Anyway, what did you expect? You have done everything in your power to create problems for the United States government during your term as governor. Did you think they were going to forget all about that?"

"I suppose if our roles were reversed, I would do the same thing."

Adam looked at his watch, then he stood up and said, "I have a meeting at one o'clock, so I have to leave. When you get the financial analysis completed, please let me know."

"You'll be the first person I'll call when I get it."

Russell Fine

XI
Becker Aerospace
May 15, 2025

Harold Becker sat at the head of the conference room table. The other five people present in the room were the leaders of his strike teams. Each of the leaders had given Harold a list of potential targets. Harold had gone over the lists carefully and selected their next target. He looked at the other people and they were obviously waiting for him to speak. He said, "I've looked at the lists each of you has given me, and I've done some research as well. I believe our next target should be the Bixby Creek Bridge on Highway 1. I selected this because I didn't want our next target to be in southern California. Additionally, I want to use some of the ordinance we received from our friends in Washington. I'm sure this will make the idiots in Sacramento believe there are at least two guerilla groups in California."

Ben Johnson, one of the Army Rangers, said, "I think that's an excellent choice. It's very sparsely traveled at night, and about fifteen pounds of C4 in the middle section will collapse at least thirty feet of the bridge. It will probably cost a few million to repair it."

Everyone at the meeting agreed with the target. They spent the next two hours planning the attack. They selected 3:00 AM on Tuesday May 20th as the date and time of the event. Harold acquired two old twenty-eight-foot box trucks for the attack. The two Army Rangers spent the weekend constructing three bombs; a big one for the bridge, and two smaller ones designed to blow up the trucks. On May 19th three vehicles left Becker Aerospace early in the morning. Two of them were the box trucks, the third vehicle was Ben Johnson's car. Once again, they created phony license plates for all the vehicles.

The route was carefully planned, staying off main highways as much as possible. They stopped three miles south of the bridge a little after 2:00 AM and pulled onto the shoulder, waiting and watching the traffic. They watched for about 15 minutes. Since no vehicles passed them from either direction, they resumed their journey. When they were about a quarter mile south of the bridge, the first truck made s sharp left turn and pulled onto the shoulder on the opposite side of the road, giving the second truck and the car just enough room to pass on the right shoulder. After the second truck and the car passed, the driver of the first truck maneuvered it into a position so it blocked traffic from both directions. The driver got out of the truck leaving the lights and motor on. He ran over and got into Ben's car.

When they were at the center of the bridge, Ben stopped his car, hopped out, and placed the bomb in the middle of the span. Then he got back into his car and stopped again about a quarter mile north of the bridge. The driver of the second truck quickly maneuvered his truck so it blocked traffic. He got out of the truck and ran over to Ben's car. After the driver was in the car, they drove another quarter of mile before Ben detonated the bombs. A few seconds later they heard the explosions, but they would have to wait until the following morning to find out the extent of the damage.

At about 8:00 AM a group of reporters were on the Capitol Building steps waiting for President Nelson to arrive. He knew they would be waiting and had rehearsed what he was going to say. His bodyguards cleared a path through the group. He ignored all questions being yelled at him, and when he got to the landing, he turned to face them. He raised his hands asking for quiet, and as soon as the reporter stopped yelling, he began to speak.

"The heinous attack perpetrated by a cowardly group of terrorists destroyed a historical, and beautiful, California landmark. Our investigators are going over the forensic evidence as we speak. I feel confident we will find the people responsible for this attack shortly, and they will pay a heavy price for this senseless act of destruction.

"We are fully committed to actions we have taken to create our new country, and no group of terrorists is going to have any effect on how we govern it. We will release more information as it becomes available. Thank you."

As soon as he finished speaking, the reporters began yelling questions again. Once more, he completely ignored them and walked into the building.

Two hours later, President Nelson was seated in his office when his secretary opened the door. Adam Peterson walked in and sat down across from President Nelson and asked, "Anything new?"

"Yeah, and it's not good. The bomb this time was made from C4, and was placed in a position on the bridge to maximize the destruction. Our engineers aren't sure the bridge can be repaired. They're still evaluating the damage. The two trucks used to block the road had fake license plates. They were actually made out of paper. There wasn't much left of the trucks to examine, but all the VIN numbers had been removed. It will be impossible to find out who owned the trucks. I'm somewhat grateful they used the trucks as barriers to prevent anyone from being injured, but I would still like to hang the bastards!"

"We discussed this before. You knew this kind of stuff would happen. I guarantee you it won't be the last attack. Do you think it was the same group that caused the power failures?"

President Nelson didn't answer immediately. He sat there, looking at Adam and fondling his right ear lobe for several seconds. Then he said, "I'm not sure. I just assumed it was a different group. They used a different explosive and this attack was hundreds of miles from the first one. The only similarity was the timing of the attack."

"Despite your promise to find the culprits quickly, I don't think that's very likely. Do you?"

"To be honest, I did when I said it. But now I'm not so sure."

"Gary, I'm sorry to change the subject, but we have to talk about the problems created by opening the border with Mexico. Our best estimate is that about nineteen thousand people crossed the border, and we're providing food, shelter, and medical care for virtually every one of them. That number is growing by about five hundred per day. If that continues, and I see nothing to slow it down, it's going to cost us hundreds of millions of dollars, and we can't afford it. Additionally, almost every illegal drug known to man is being openly sold on the streets in every major city. The police in San Diego estimated that three tons of drugs are crossing the border every day. We have to do something."

"Are you telling me we have to shut the border again? I won't do that. I promised that anyone who wants to come to California is welcome, and I intend to keep that promise."

"I completely understand how you feel, but are you ready to welcome the drug smugglers too? If the situation at the border is allowed to continue, we'll find ourselves in deep financial trouble."

"Do you have a suggestion?

Adam replied, "I do, but you won't like it. I think we have to inspect all vehicles crossing the border and check them for drugs, and we should probably limit the number of people who can cross the border each day. I'm sure you're aware that we have already seen a twenty percent increase in drug related admissions at our hospitals, and that's going to get worse. And while we are speaking about hospitals; I've had reports from the people I know who work at our hospitals and they told me that a majority of the staff are ready to revolt. They said that there are too many patients, the hours are too long, and they are unable to provide adequate care for them. What they're not saying publicly is that the hours are too long, the pay is too low, and the situation is being exacerbated by the drug shortages that are occurring at almost every hospital. Do you realize the average wait time in our hospital emergency rooms is in excess of ten hours!"

President Nelson's facial expression changed. He was obviously angry. He screamed, "Yeah, I know that, but what the hell can I do about it? I won't put guards on our border again!"

"Calm down Gary. If you don't want to limit the number of people crossing the border, can't we at least check for drugs?"

"I don't see how we could do that without putting guards on the border again."

"I think the people would be okay with having guards again, as long as all they were doing is checking for drugs."

President Nelson sighed deeply and said, "I suppose we have no choice. You know, I'm not sure I want this job. I don't like the decisions I have to make."

"So far you are running unopposed in the election. If you're going to drop out, you have to do it soon, because we have to find a replacement."

"I think you should be my replacement."

"I'm not a politician, I'm a business man."

"You know, you're really full of shit. You're more of a politician than I've ever been. The only difference is, you want to control things in the background. But I think this is your opportunity to lead California into a bright new future."

Adam smiled when he said, "Do you want to be my campaign manager? You sound like it already."

"I think I'll pass on that opportunity. But I will make a decision regarding the election in the next few days."

"Okay, please take care of the situation at the border. I'll be back in few days."

As soon as Adam left, President Nelson picked up his phone and asked Tony, his chief of staff, to come into his office.

Tony appeared a few minutes later. He asked as he walked into the office, "What's up?"

"I really don't want to do this, but we have to stop the drug smuggling from Mexico. I want you to set up a system to check every person and every vehicle crossing the border for drugs."

"Yes sir, I understand. I'm sure we have trained dogs to do that. I think we can get that implemented within forty-eight hours. We should also postpone demolition of the border walls until this situation is resolved."

"I suppose so. Please take care of that too, and set up a news briefing at 4:00."

"Yes, sir."

At the allotted time, President Nelson stepped up to the podium in the press room and began, "I wanted to make you aware of two situations. First, I'm sorry to report that the Bixby Bridge will have to be demolished and rebuilt. That process will take a year and will cost about fifteen million dollars. We realize that many people are dependent on the Pacific Coast Highway for their daily commute, and I promise we will complete the work as quickly as possible. Unfortunately, we haven't made any progress yet in identifying the culprits, but that task will continue.

"I also want to make you aware of a situation at our border with Mexico. In the few weeks since we became an independent country, more than nineteen thousand immigrants have crossed the border. This has created a temporary problem at some hospitals, but we expect that situation to be resolved shortly. However, in addition to people crossing the border, the Mexican drug cartels are taking advantage of our open border. I have received estimates that approximately three tons of drugs are coming into California every day. I didn't want to do this, but I have no choice. Within forty-eight hours we will begin checking all people and vehicles that cross our border for drugs. If we find drugs on a vehicle, the vehicle will be forfeited, and the driver and passengers will be arrested. If we find drugs on an individual, that person will be arrested. The minimum sentence for drug smuggling is two years in jail, and in addition, we will make it a very unpleasant two years.

"We must stop the flow of illegal drugs. In the last two weeks the number of drug related hospital admissions has increased by ten percent. We're working with the Mexican government to resolve the problem, but we can't wait for their assistance. So, we are postponing the demolition of existing border walls until this situation has been resolved.

"My chief of staff will be here in a few moments to answer any questions. Thank you for your time."

XII
California
May, 2025

During the entire month, streams of immigrants crossed California's southern border. By the end of the month, California had more than twenty thousand new residents, and that number was growing by five hundred per day. None of them had jobs, or money, and only a few had arranged for a place to live. The buses were there every day, ready to take them to whatever community was willing to accept them, but that number was dwindling.

Virtually every city south of Los Angeles was unable to accept any new immigrants, so they started to take them to cities in central California. But many of the cities refused to accept them. The residents of that part of the country were far more conservative than those living along the coast. They were already unhappy with the decision to make California an independent country, and now they're being asked to pay a large portion of the expenses associated with housing the new immigrants.

Although the cities along the coast were all for independence and open borders, many of those cities simply didn't want large groups of poor immigrants messing up their neighborhoods.

By the end of May, only Los Angeles, San Francisco, Sacramento, and Stockton were willing to accept them.

During May, California fully implemented their plan to charge fees for all goods entering the United States. Every truck and railroad car leaving California was required to have a list of every item they were transporting and the retail value of the item. Customs agents spot checked trucks and railway cars. If the list was found to be incorrect, the truck or railway car was impounded. Truckers tried to avoid the checkpoints by travelling on little used country highways to cross into Nevada, Arizona, and Oregon. The move was expected and the Highway Patrol set up temporary checkpoints on many of these roads. During the month, two hundred sixty-one truck drivers were arrested and their trucks and the contents became the property of California.

These fees brought in about twenty-four million dollars during May. It was expected that by September that number would be close to one hundred million dollars.

During May, most of the medical community became incensed with the new regulations. They were now required to work eighty-hour weeks, for much less money than they were making before. Due to overcrowding, many of the hospitals and clinics were unable to maintain their facilities properly, and many began to look like facilities in third world countries.

The plan to check incoming vehicles and people for drugs was quickly implemented, and it proved to be a total failure. After the first few shipments were intercepted, the drug cartels quickly realized what was happening and began shipping drugs into California by using small boats. They could easily stop on any beach in southern California and unload their cargo. Prior to becoming an independent country, the California coast was patrolled by United States Coast Guard vessels. But, since California had nothing equivalent to the Coast Guard, the drug boats moved freely between Mexico and California.

By the end of the month, doctors and nurses who didn't own homes began to leave California by the hundreds. Every hospital in the state was desperately short of medical personnel, and the crowds at emergency rooms had not dwindled. Both California residents and the new immigrants were unable to get emergency medical care in a reasonable amount of time. In some cases, people had to wait more than twenty-four hours to be seen.

Although the number of new immigrants dropped after the first few days the border was opened, it had risen to more than a thousand per day by the end of May. The government was forced to set up tent cities along the border to house the immigrants. There were food and water shortages, limited sanitary facilities, and in general conditions were not much better than they were in their home countries.

President Nelson was completely unable to cope with the situation. In a televised speech on May 28, 2025, he told the residents of California he was withdrawing his name from the ballot in the election that was scheduled for June 24th. He said he believed Adam Peterson should be the first elected President of California.

Russell Fine

XIII
Becker Aerospace
June 2, 2025

Harold Becker was in his conference room meeting with his strike team leaders. He said, "We all know that California is in serious trouble. They can't seem to do anything right. Everything they try fails. They opened the border with Mexico, and now we have more immigrants than we can handle, illegal drugs are both easier to get and less expensive, and because our new residents are flooding hospital emergency rooms, people are dying in every emergency room in the country due to personnel shortages. I found it humorous that when they tried to start construction to rebuild the Bixby Bridge, a group of environmentalists filed a suit to prevent the construction, and apparently construction has been halted for an indefinite amount of time. I think it's time we stepped up our game. I want the next target to be one that makes peoples' lives miserable for weeks or months. Any suggestions?"

Carl Hollings said, "Harold, I think that given a few months, California will collapse on its own. I'm not sure we have to do anything more. It looks like we'll be broke in a month or two."

Harold looked at Carl and replied, "I wish that were true, but I've heard a rumor that they have access to about three hundred billion dollars in cash. I suspect that the helping hand is coming from China. If the rumor is correct, we have to act now, because we want the Chinese to know that helping California with large amounts of cash is a really bad investment. I think the best way to do that is with increased acts of insurrection."

"Do you think the money is a gift, or do they want something in return?" Carl asked.

"Nobody gives away that much money. There has to be some ulterior motive. If the money is a loan, and California is unable to pay it back, I'm sure they will want something instead."

"I think we should give them San Francisco. I, for one, won't miss it. Actually, we could give them Oakland and Berkley too."

Several people in the room laughed, but Harold did not. "This situation is not a joke. If the Chinese get a foot hold in

47

California, they will quickly take over the entire country. We have no Army to stop them," he said.

Carl responded, "You're right, of course. But I don't think there are enough of us to do what you suggest."

"There must be other insurgent groups we aren't aware of. I'll try to find out in the next few days. In any case, let's meet again in the three days. Please try to pick some potential targets.

The following morning Harold received a call from Roy Stuart. After a brief greeting Roy said, "Harold, we heard a rumor, and if it's true, it's a major concern for us. As you know, we have cut California out of the national power grid, and they are now totally dependent on the power generating facilities inside the country. All indications are that it's going to be a very hot summer, causing substantially increased demand for electricity. Apparently, Adam Peterson just returned from a meeting in China to discuss solutions to California's power shortage. I'm sure you're aware that Diablo Canyon was scheduled to be closed by the end of this year. However, instead of closing it, they have made a deal with China to increase the capacity of the plant by a minimum of fifty percent. Additionally, there was a discussion about restarting San Onofre. Apparently, the equipment, which was supposed to be scrapped ten years ago, is still there, and the Chinese have promised they can make the plant operational again in less than eighteen months."

"So, China will soon have a presence in California. I was afraid that might happen. What do you want me to do?"

"We would like you to make sure that restarting San Onofre isn't an option."

"We can't blow it up. They are storing tons of radioactive waste there. I won't do anything that has a potential to harm anyone."

"I realize that, and I completely agree. However, we have some engineers looking at the plant designs. They are looking for something you can do that would increase the startup time by a year or two. I'll keep you informed."

"Okay, that seems reasonable."

"One more thing. We are keeping constant, and very discrete surveillance, on your facility. We know that currently your phone is not tapped and currently nobody is spying on you, but we can't be sure it will stay that way. We have to be able to speak to each other freely. Tomorrow, someone will stop by your office and drop off a portable scrambler. Please install it immediately. The instructions will be self-explanatory."

"Is anything being done about Diablo Canyon?"

"Yes, there is another group, similar to yours, but larger, based near Eureka. They have a plan for Diablo Canyon."

"Okay, I don't want to know what it is. I would rather be surprised."

"I wouldn't have told you more anyway. I'll call you again in few days."

Harold was worried. So far, he was able to carry out his attacks in areas that were unprotected. That would not be the case with San Onofre. And, he was positive that once the Chinese arrived, it would probably be impossible to get within a mile or two of the place. If they were going to act, it would have to done soon.

Russell Fine

XIV
Sacramento
June 5, 2025

President Nelson and Adam Peterson were alone in Nelson's office. Gary said, "Adam, it's nice to have you back. I hope you're ready to take over this job next month. It's far more difficult and exasperating than I ever thought possible. I don't know how you're going to handle it."

"It won't be easy, but I think our new friends are going to help with some of our problems. They promised to send a fleet of boats to patrol our coast to prevent drug smuggling, and they will use whatever force is required to stop the smugglers. They have also agreed to supply us with doctors and nurses to alleviate the shortage."

"That will be a big help, but are we sure we're ready to cozy up to the Chinese? They aren't doing this for us because they're nice people who only want to help. You know they want something. Do you have any idea what it is?"

Adam sighed deeply, and said, "You're right, of course, but at this point we have no choice. Have you seen the weather forecast? Tomorrow it will be at least ninety-seven degrees in the San Fernando Valley. Our electrical grid will not be able to handle the load. There are going to be rolling blackouts, and the people are going to be really pissed off. We have to have a plan to deal with the situation. I'm not pleased with the plan, but it's the quickest way to get us the power we need. When the environmentalists find out what the plans are for San Onofre and Diablo Canyon, they are going to go crazy. There will be marches, lawsuits, and probably death threats, but we can't let them stop us."

"You do realize that whatever you do, at least half the people in California will hate you."

"Yeah, but I want our country to succeed, and that's going to require making tough choices. I'll have to go on television and tell people what we're doing, and why we are doing it. I can only hope they'll understand."

"You better do it soon."

Adam laughed a little and said, "It's already been arranged. I think tomorrow morning will be soon enough."

At eight o'clock the following morning, Adam was seated at his desk. All the major news organizations were there and they were waiting for Adam to speak. He was slightly nervous, although he had been interviewed several times since President Nelson withdrew his name from consideration to become the first elected President of California and suggested Adam as his replacement. This was the first time Adam was giving a prepared speech. He was much more comfortable speaking to small groups, but he knew this was just going to be the first of many speeches he would be required to make.

Upon a signal from the director he began speaking, "Good morning. Although I have not taken over for President Nelson yet, I wanted to speak to the people of California regarding our current circumstances. I believe it's very important to keep all of you informed. The process of starting a new country is complex, and fraught with problems. However, I believe that with the help of some new friends, these problems will be resolved fairly quickly.

"The primary reason I wanted to speak to you this morning is because many of you in the southern and central sections of our country will be experiencing abnormally warm temperatures this afternoon. I'm sorry to inform you that our electric utilities will not be able to meet the demand for electric power. To prevent a major failure in our electrical grid, there will be rolling blackouts. These blackouts have been scheduled, and none will last more than an hour. If your area is affected, you will receive an automated text message within the next two hours. These blackouts will continue for the next four days. At that time, a significant change in the weather is expected.

"Prior to withdrawing from the United States, we were able to purchase additional power from utilities in other states when needed, but we have been cut off from the United States electrical grid and we're on our own. We do have a solution for this problem, although it will take about eighteen months to resolve. The Diablo Canyon nuclear power station was going to be retired this year. That will not happen, instead we will be increasing its capacity substantially, and it will remain online for the foreseeable future.

The California Experiment

The San Onofre power station, which was decommissioned thirteen years ago, will be reactivated. Once this power station is back online, we will have sufficient electrical power to prevent the need for rolling blackouts. For those of you concerned with the safety of these facilities, I can assure you that safety will not be an issue. We will be installing the safest, most modern, and efficient equipment available.

"The next problem I want to discuss with you is the increased presence of drugs in California. Since we opened our border with Mexico, the Mexican drug cartels have attempted to take advantage of our open border and bring tons of illicit drugs here. In the past sixty days the availability of these drugs has increased substantially, and the prices have dropped by almost fifty percent. To stop the flow of drugs, we set up border checkpoints for all incoming vehicles. This helped, but only for a few days. The cartels quickly realized what we were doing, and now they're shipping the drugs in small boats that can stop at almost any beach and unload their poison. Since we don't have the ability to protect our shoreline from these criminals, we are currently powerless to stop them. However, this problem will be addressed shortly. Within a week, more than fifty heavily armed, high speed boats, complete with crews, will be arriving and begin patrolling our shoreline.

"The last issue I want to tell you about is the shortage of adequate medical personnel at our hospitals. Since we opened our border, almost fifty thousand people have crossed and became residents of California. We welcomed them here as many have received inadequate medical care in their home countries and they are in desperate need of professional medical help. I feel we must provide them with the help they need, but we need additional doctors and nurses to do that. I'm happy to announce that over the next sixty days, hundreds of doctors and nurses will be arriving to help. Their arrival will allow us to significantly reduce the wait time to see a medical professional in our hospital emergency rooms.

"All of this assistance is coming from a single source. I just returned from a trip to Beijing, where I spent several days meeting with Chinese leaders. The result of those meetings was; China will supply the people and equipment needed to resolve our electrical problems, the boats and crews to stop the flow of drugs, and the medical personnel we need for our hospitals. In exchange, we agreed to eliminate all tariffs on Chinese imports, and wherever possible, purchase Chinese products for our needs.

"I hope you all believe, as I do, that these actions are a step in the right direction, and the people of California will benefit as a result. Thank you for your time."

The reaction to the speech was swift, and mostly negative. Within hours three law suits were filed to stop the planned work at San Onofre and Diablo Canyon. Several more were filed to terminate the agreement with China. By the end of the day, Adam Peterson, who had been running unopposed for President of California, suddenly found himself with three opponents. Apparently, the only people happy with the plan were the people in the southern part of the state that were now subjected to daily rolling power outages.

The following morning, President Nelson and Adam Peterson met with the Chief Justice of The California Supreme Court. As a result of that meeting, the decision was made that the pending law suits would not be heard by the lower courts. They would be heard immediately by the Supreme Court. This gave the plaintiffs virtually no time to prepare their cases. They wanted to file complaints, but there was no court to file them with. Every suit was dismissed by the Supreme Court by June 12, 2025.

The election was scheduled on June 24, 2025. Adam Peterson won with fifty-four percent of the vote. He was scheduled to assume the position of President on June 30, 2025. By coincidence, that was the same day the Chinese boats began to patrol the California coast line.

In addition to the boats, more than two hundred drones were launched. Their job was to monitor every beach south of Long Beach. Every boat on the water was monitored. Shortly after 10:00 PM that evening, a thirty-five-foot boat was detected moving north along the coast at about thirty knots. It was running without navigation lights. A patrol boat was dispatched to intercept it. When the patrol boat was within a half mile of the offending craft, attempts were made to hail the boat in both English and Spanish. As a result, the boat increased their speed to almost fifty knots in an attempt to outrun the patrol boat. The patrol issued a warning in both languages informing them that if they didn't stop, their boat would be destroyed. The warning was ignored. A drone about fifty yards behind fired an explosive shell at the boat. The shell was designed to explode on impact. The boat was instantly engulfed in flames and sank within minutes. It was about three miles off shore. The patrol boat never even made an attempt to look for survivors.

During the night, two more boats that were presumed to belong to drug smugglers were sunk as well. When the information regarding the sunken boats became public knowledge, a small, but vocal minority, protested the actions taken by the Chinese. Their complaint was that the people in the boat should have been arrested, not murdered.

The next night, two more suspected smuggling boats were destroyed. After that, the Mexican cartels realized they had to find another way to get their drugs into California.

By early July, the promised medical personal began to arrive. They all spoke at least some English, and a few even spoke Spanish. They were immediately dispatched to hospitals along the Mexican border. They were housed in local hotels and motels, which were thrilled to get the business. Tourism had dropped by almost ninety percent since California declared its independence.

Also, in early July, Chinese troops began to arrive. Their job was to protect Diablo Canyon and San Onofre. By July 7, 2025 there were about one thousand heavily armed troops at each facility. There were fences already in place around both power stations, but the fence around San Onofre was in need of repair. That task was completed almost immediately, and every inch of the perimeter of each facility was under constant surveillance.

Russell Fine

XV
Becker Aerospace
July 11, 2025

Harold sat at his desk reading the news on his computer. The headline story was about a group of environmental terrorists that attempted to break into the Diablo Canyon power station. They were carrying explosives that were detonated during the attack on the power station. The resulting explosion killed all of the terrorists, and they never managed to penetrate the perimeter fence.

Harold read the article twice. He really wanted to speak with Roy Stuart. Their last conversation was more than a month ago, but he knew there was no way for him to initiate the call. Later that afternoon he received a cryptic message. Imbedded in the message was the code that was needed to descramble the phone.

The next morning, he entered the code into the phone which rang at precisely 10:00 AM. Harold answered with a simple, "Good morning."

"Good morning, Harold. Obviously, you got my message. I know it's been a while since we last spoke, but I thought you might be concerned about the reported failure of the attack on Diablo Canyon. I wanted you to know it was not a failure, although we were not expecting two of our operatives to be killed. Their job was to create a diversion which allowed four other people to enter the premises, do their job, and get out. That part of the plan worked perfectly."

Harold asked, "What was their job?"

"I can't discuss that with you. I'm sure you realize that. Even though this conversation can't be monitored, there's always a possibility that you, or a member of your team, will be caught. You can't tell the Chinese what you don't know."

"I understand. I shouldn't have asked. I'm sure you realize that there are two thousand armed Chinese soldiers in California right now, not including the ones that are on the patrol boats. Were you aware that would happen?"

"We didn't know the exact number, and we still don't, but we weren't surprised. We are almost ready with a plan for your operation. We had to design and build some devices. They should be ready in about a week. However, I think it's time for a few simple attacks just to get their attention."

"We can do that. My guys are anxious. They're tired of waiting. Did you have anything specific mind?"

"I think you should hit gasoline supplies, and perhaps the aqueduct."

"I told you before, I won't do anything that has the potential to hurt our people. So, the aqueduct is not a target. That being said, I have no problem making them uncomfortable. There are several major refineries within a hundred miles from here. They should be easy targets, but we can't blow them up. We have to find a way to put them out of commission for a month or two."

Roy was silent for a few moments. Then he asked, "How does the crude oil get to the refinery?"

"I'm sure it arrives by pipeline."

"Do you know where the pipelines are?"

"No, not exactly, but I'm positive I can find out. What do you have in mind?"

"Several years ago, we developed a chemical that, when added to crude oil, alters the chemical composition of the crude, which makes it impossible to refine. Once they begin the refining process, the oil turns into a thick gum-like substance that would have to be cleaned out by hand."

"That would probably knock out the refineries for a few weeks at least. How do I get the chemical?"

"I'll arrange it. You should have it in a few days. While you're waiting, find some remote area where you can get to the pipelines."

"Okay, call me again in week or so. By then, our plans will be set."

"I'll call you next week."

The price of gasoline had increased by almost $2.00 per gallon since California declared its independence. Over the previous ten years, the environmentalists had forced the closure of more than seventy-five percent of the oil drilling facilities in the state. As a result, California refineries had contracts with most of the crude oil producers in the United States, but those contracts were cancelled when California became independent. The gasoline companies found new sources of crude oil, but the price was substantially higher than what they had been paying before, so those price increases were passed on to the California consumers.

Harold immediately set up a meeting with his leaders. When they arrived in the conference room, Harold gave them the details of his conversation with Roy and told them what their next mission would be. He asked them to research pipeline locations and select the areas that would be the easiest to hit.

The following afternoon, Carl Hollings knocked lightly on Harold's open door. Harold looked up from what he was reading and said, "Hi Carl, come on in."

Carl walked in and sat across from Harold. He said, "I think we found our targets. There are three refineries in Wilmington. Between them they refine about three hundred twenty thousand barrels of crude oil per day. There's also the Chevron refinery in El Segundo. They refine about two hundred seventy-five thousand barrels per day. All these refineries receive their crude oil by pipeline. We've already located likely target areas."

"Good work Carl, that was fast. Remember, this plan won't work if sabotage is suspected."

"We know that, but until we find out how the chemical has to be injected into the pipeline, we can't finish our plans."

"Yeah, I realize that. We should have the answer in a few days."

"Have you thought about what will happen to the price of gas if we do this? I'll bet the price goes over ten dollars a gallon. The people will go nuts."

"I'm counting on that. Maybe it will force the morons in Sacramento to do something right for a change, like allow some new oil rigs to go up so we'll be less dependent on imports."

"I wouldn't hold my breath waiting for that," Carl said with a smile, "but it's a nice thought."

Three days later, a truck delivered four large cartons to the Becker Aerospace facility. Since they were basically out of business, the delivery was a surprise. Nobody, except Harold and

Carl, were aware of the delivery. The cartons were labeled "*machine parts*" and each carton weighed one hundred twenty-five pounds. Carl opened one of the cartons. Inside were boxes of airplane parts. Carl began to remove the boxes, and after he had emptied about a third of the carton, he discovered another carton inside that was surrounded by smaller boxes of airplane parts. He lifted the inside carton and put it on a work table. When he opened it, he found a plastic container about the size of a five-gallon paint can. Attached to the top was a rubber hose about six feet long. On the other end was a device that looked like a very large pistol.

Carl called Harold and asked him to come over to the loading dock. Harold arrived a few minutes later and spent several minutes examining the device Carl had found in the box. He said, "I'm sure this is one of the devices we were expecting. I suspect the thing at the end of the hose is designed to pierce the pipeline. Can I assume there were no instructions?"

"There was nothing in the box except this contraption. We should probably find out how to use it before our mission."

"I think it's fairly intuitive, but I'm sure we'll hear from Roy shortly. I'll ask him. In the meantime, open the other cartons. Put the airplane parts into stock, and hide the devices."

"Will do."

Harold didn't have to wait long for Roy's call. He received a coded message an hour later, and a half hour after that the phone rang.

"Hi Harold, I know you received your shipment. Did you find the special items I sent?'

"Yes, of course. I like the way the shipment was packaged. Even if the cartons were inspected, I doubt they would have found the primary items."

"That was our plan, but they are much more careful with material leaving California than things coming in. Do you have any questions?"

"Well, yeah. There were no instructions."

"It's very simple. You turn on the device, press the barrel of the gun against the pipeline, and pull the trigger. There are sensors on the tip of the barrel that analyze the pipeline material. Pipelines are typically made out of plastic, but some are steel. So, before the device can do its job properly, it has to know the composition of the material it's about to puncture. Once the analysis is finished, a green light will glow faintly. Then you release the trigger, make sure the barrel is still pressed firmly against the pipeline and pull the trigger again. The device will puncture the pipeline and attach itself firmly to it. The device inserts a small tube into the pipeline. As the oil moves over the tube, a vacuum is created which sucks the chemical out of the container. It will take between two and three hours for the contents to be sucked into the pipeline, but you don't have to wait. As soon as it's attached, your people can leave."

"That seems simple enough. When do you want us to do it?"

"Within forty-eight hours if that's possible. To maximize the impact, all four pipelines must be hit the same day."

"Okay, we've already selected the areas where the pipelines are most vulnerable, and we've been discretely watching them for the last three days."

"Good, just don't get caught."

"Aren't they going to realize the United States government is involved when they find the devices?"

"Possibly, but these devices were built by a California company. So, we'll simply deny any involvement and tell them to look at home for their terrorists."

"Wouldn't it make more sense to remove the devices after the chemicals have been sucked into the pipeline?"

"Once the device is attached, it can't be removed. You would have to cut the pipeline, and that would create a noticeable decrease in pressure, which would trigger an alarm."

"Okay, I understand now. I'm sure you'll know if we're successful."

"Yeah, I'm fairly sure it'll make the news all over the world. Good luck, Harold."

Two days later the four strike teams left Becker Aerospace. They arrived at their assigned targets and were in position by 11:00 PM. At 11:05 the devices were attached to the pipeline, and by 11:15 they were all on their way home.

The chemical would not react with the crude oil until it reached a temperature of 135 degrees F. When that happened, the chemical would cause all the crude oil to become almost solid in a matter of seconds. As the heat increased, the crude would become more solid. The automatic safety systems in the refineries would be triggered and the refineries would be shut down.

By 9:00 AM the following morning, all four of the targeted refineries had shut down. But it was almost 11:00 AM before the refinery operators realized that four of them had shut down. It was obviously some form of sabotage, but they had no idea how four refineries could be sabotaged at the same time.

By noon, Adam Peterson was aware of the problem. He made the decision to keep the situation secret for the time being. He was hoping the refineries would find the problem and resolve it quickly. He knew there were sufficient gasoline stocks to last for fifteen days, so as long as the problem was resolved before they ran out of gas, there would be no need to panic the public.

He called his assistant, Ellen Miller, into his office and explained the situation to her. Then he asked her to get down to the LA area and report back to him as soon as she had anything to report.

Three hours later, Ellen was in a large office at the Chevron refinery in El Segundo. The man sitting behind the desk rose from his chair and said, "Good morning, Ms. Miller. My name is Brian Wilson, I'm the superintendent of this facility."

He paused for a moment and said, somewhat angrily, "The situation is very serious. Something turned the crude into a solid block. It will probably take at least a month for the repairs. This was obviously some form of sabotage. Something happened to the crude while it was in the pipeline. We've never seen anything like it. We have crews inspecting the pipeline now, but even if they locate the problem, it won't be of much help. We already know what needs to be done."

"That's really bad news. We'll be out gas for the public in two weeks."

"I'm sorry to say it will take less time than that for the public to realize there's a problem. By this evening they'll realize we're shut down. There will be no visible fires. As the word spreads that four refineries are out of commission, there will be mass panic."

"I hadn't thought about that." Ellen sighed deeply and said, "I'd better call President Peterson and let him know."

Ellen took her cell phone out of her purse and called Adam on his personal phone. When he answered, she told him the what she had learned. He replied, "The bad news never stops, does it? Please arrange a news conference tomorrow morning at 9:00 AM. I will have to give another speech the public won't like."

Ellen said, "I'm sorry, sir. I'll take care of the news conference. I'll see you in the office in the morning."

Ellen put the phone back in her purse. She was about to thank Mr. Wilson for his time when his phone rang. He answered it, then said nothing for almost a minute. As he listened, the expression on his face changed. He was obviously very upset by what was being said. Then he said, "Thank you for the information." He hung up the phone, and obviously angry again, said, "Ms. Miller, the four pipelines leading to the four affected refineries each had some type of device attached that dispensed something into the pipeline which modified the composition of the crude oil. Their best guess is the substance causes the crude to solidify when it's heated. Simply put, I suspect the pipelines may have to be replaced, and that could take up to a year. That means, once we get back in operation, we'll have to use trucks to transport the crude from the ships to the refineries. That'll reduce our output by forty or fifty percent."

Ellen realized immediately how this news was going to affect the public. She stood up and thanked Mr. Wilson for his time, and went back to her waiting limo. As soon as she was inside, she called Adam again. When Adam answered she told him about her last conversation with Mr. Wilson. She had seldom heard Adam get that upset; all she could hear was his harsh breathing for a while. When he finally spoke, he said, trying to control his anger, "I'd like to personally torture the assholes responsible for this. I have to think about this situation. If you have any ideas, please let me know. I'll see you in the morning."

The next morning, Ellen arrived at the office a few minutes before seven. She was surprised to find that Adam was already there.

When she walked into his office he looked up, smiled weakly, and said "Good morning. That's a wish, not a statement. I have been here for a couple of hours trying to figure out what I'm going to say. Any suggestions?"

"You're not a politician, and a very bad liar. Just tell them the truth."

"Yeah, that was my thought too. I guess I'll spend the next hour deciding what I'm going to say.

By 8:45 the cameras were set up in Adam's office, and at 9:00 he began to speak.

"Before I became President of California, I promised that if I was elected, I would always tell you the truth. I'm sorry to be the bearer of bad news, but that goes with the job.

"Two days ago, four crude oil pipelines in the southern part of our country were sabotaged. A chemical was introduced into the pipelines causing the crude oil to become a solid mass when heated. The result was devastating. The four major refineries that were on the receiving ends of the pipelines were severely damaged, and the time to get them back online is unknown. The original estimates were a month, but it may take longer than that. The damage to the pipeline will take far longer to repair. The latest estimate I have is that it may take up to a year. Even after the refineries are back in operation, they will not be able to operate at peak capacity because the crude oil processed will have to be delivered by tanker truck.

"We have a strategic gasoline reserve, which I will release immediately. We believe we may be able to increase output from the refineries still in operation. Additionally, we'll begin purchasing refined gasoline from other countries. It's my hope that these actions will keep the supply steady until the affected refineries are operating at capacity again.

"I know unscrupulous gas stations will probably try to raise their prices. To prevent that, I'm issuing an executive order that caps gas station profits on gasoline sales at ten cents per gallon. Anyone caught price gouging will be severely fined. Repeat offences will result in forfeiture of their facility.

"To help minimize the effects of the potential gasoline shortages, I'm asking everyone to limit unnecessary trips and carpool when possible. Pretend the cost of a gallon of gas is more than ten dollars, and act accordingly.

"This is still a fluid situation. As more information becomes available, we'll immediately notify the public.

"Thank you for your time this morning. I will speak to you again soon."

Russell Fine

XVI
Washington, D.C.
July 14, 2025

President Haskell was seated at her desk. Facing her was Roy Stuart. She said, "Good morning, Roy. You requested this meeting. What's up?"

"I wanted to make sure you were aware of the relationship between California and China. I came across some information you may not be aware of."

"I know about the power stations, the medical personnel, and the beach security patrols. Is there something else?"

"Yes, according to my source, after the refineries and pipeline were damaged, President Peterson met with a delegation from China. The purpose of the meeting was to discuss the possibility of the Chinese suppling the personnel necessary to protect the other refineries and pipelines in California. After several hours of discussion, the Chinese agreed to provide the protection Peterson requested, in exchange for allowing China to set up a military base in California. Apparently, Peterson has not made a decision yet.

"This level of involvement between California and the Chinese was completely unexpected. There are already more than two thousand Chinese military personnel in California, and I don't think we want to take any action that would push Peterson into an agreement with the Chinese."

She paused for a moment and said, "I probably shouldn't ask, but were you responsible for the damaged refineries?"

"You're right, you shouldn't ask."

President Haskell, deep in thought, rubbed her fingers lightly over her chin. Finally, she spoke, "I think we need to have a meeting with the Chinese Ambassador to discuss this situation. I'll have the State Department set it up. In the interim, please verify the information you have."

"Yes, I'll do that. But we can't allow a Chinese military base in California."

"I agree, but we may be powerless to stop it."

Roy was silent for a few seconds. Then he replied, "We may not be as powerless as you think. So far, we have not interfered with California access to water rights from the Colorado River. What if we threaten to cut off their water if they don't stop playing nice with the Chinese?"

"That's not a bad idea. I don't think it's anything we would actually do, but it may be a viable threat. Let's find out what would be needed to cut off their water and let me know."

"Of course. I'll get on it this morning."

After Roy left her office, President Haskell called the Secretary of State, Dennis Crenshaw, and asked him to set up a meeting with the Chinese Ambassador. They briefly discussed the purpose of the meeting, and Secretary Crenshaw said he would try to set it up for the following morning.

President Haskell was thinking about what she was going to say to the Chinese Ambassador when her phone rang. She answered it and her assistant said that President Peterson wanted to speak with her. She was surprised, to say the least. The United States refused to acknowledge that California was a separate country, and there had been only minimal communications between the two governments. She told her assistant to put the call through.

"Good morning, President Peterson. I was just thinking about you. What prompted this call?"

"Madam President, is the United States responsible for the destruction of four crude oil pipelines and causing severe damage to four of our refineries?"

"That's rather blunt, and not very diplomatic. However, I can tell you that I have no knowledge of any such actions."

"Do you know what all of the people who work for you do? Could one of them be responsible?"

"President Peterson, do you know what all of the people who work for you do? I'm sure you don't, and I don't know what all of people who work for the United States do either. I suggest you look at California based terrorist groups before you start accusing the United States of taking covert actions inside California."

"I believe the people of California are firmly behind our separation from the United States, and they would not take any action that would damage our local resources."

"Then you are incredibly naïve. However, this is probably not the best time to discuss that. I am aware you are considering allowing the Chinese to set up a military base in California. I would suggest that you don't do that."

"Is that a threat? Are you going to invade California?"

"No, President Peterson. I have no intention of invading California. However, I will tell you that if you allow the Chinese to set up a military base, I will take immediate action to cut off the water supply to Southern California."

President Peterson said nothing for several seconds. When he spoke again there was a note of hostility in his voice, "So, you are threating us. I know you have the power to cut off our water supplies, but I don't believe you would put millions of people at risk over something so insignificant."

"I don't consider a Chinese military base next to the United States insignificant. I plan on voicing my concerns with the Chinese Ambassador in the morning."

President Peterson said, "Thank you for speaking with me, Madam President," and he abruptly ended the connection.

President Haskell hung up her phone and thought it went rather badly, but she was sure she got her point across.

At 10:30 the following morning, the President's assistant knocked on the door to the Oval Office, opened it slightly, and said, "Secretary Crenshaw and the Chinese Ambassador are here to see you".

"Please show them in."

The two men walked into the room. President Haskell said, "Mr. Ambassador, it is a pleasure to meet you." Then she reached forward and shook his hand and they smiled at each other. Then motioning to one of the couches in the room she said, "Please make yourself comfortable. Would you like some coffee or tea?"

They both declined and sat down. President Haskell sat on the couch opposite them and said, "Mr. Ambassador, I asked you here today because I'm very concerned about the situation in

California. I realize you have offered them some assistance in several areas where their government was unable to cope with some serious situations. Making sure they can supply their citizens with sufficient electrical energy is very important, and they created the shortage of medical personnel through their own inept policies. However, I'm sure President Peterson is grateful for the assistance your country has provided. Additionally, preventing illegal drugs from entering California is a task we all appreciate."

"Thank you, Madam President. We are pleased you approve of our efforts to assist them. This is a difficult time for California and we are pleased to help where we can. Additionally, there are more than two million citizens of Chinese descent living in California and we feel an obligation to protect them."

"I understand. For the past seven years our mutually beneficial relationship has grown, and I don't want to do anything that hurts our friendship, but I heard something yesterday that deeply disturbed me."

"Please tell me what disturbed you."

"I know terrorists destroyed four crude oil pipelines and caused severe damage to the associated refineries. I understand the need to protect their national resources, and I know California does not have the necessary resources. I was told that they asked your country to provide security for the remaining refineries, and China agreed in exchange for being allowed to build a military base there. I hope what I heard was just a rumor, but I would like to hear what you have to say about this situation."

"Madam President, are you concerned for the safety of the United States if we build a military base in California?"

"Yes, Mr. Ambassador, I am very concerned. At the request of China, we refrained from building a military base in Taiwan. Now I'm asking you for the same courtesy."

"Needless to say, this is not my decision. However, I will certainly make my government aware of your concerns."

"Thank you. I appreciate that. Thank you for coming on such short notice."

"It was a pleasure to meet with you, Madam President."

The two men left the office together. A few minutes later Dennis Crenshaw returned. He said, "Madam President, I think you upset the Chinese Ambassador. I'm positive he expected you to be a pushover. I think you handled that situation perfectly. Mentioning Taiwan was a stroke of genius."

"Do you think they'll abandon the idea of having a base in California?"

"It's too soon to tell. You shook them up a little, but I expect they won't give up that easily."

"I'm pushing both sides to end this deal before it happens. I told President Peterson that if he permits the Chinese to establish a military base California, I would cut off their access to water from the Colorado River."

"I'll bet that got his attention."

"Peterson said he didn't believe I would do it."

"Would you?"

"I've been thinking about this since my conversation with Peterson yesterday. California took property that was worth several billion dollars. They tried to blackmail us too. I decided that I'm not going to sit idly by while they try to screw us again. So, to answer your question; yes."

"I think you should make the public aware of what's going on."

"I agree, but we have to see how this plays out first."

"I'll keep you informed."

"Thanks, Dennis."

Russell Fine

XVII
97 Miles West of Los Angeles
July 17, 2025

At 7:42 AM the sea floor began to crumble as an 8.1 quake struck a minor fault line. The quake lasted for almost two minutes. By that time the sea floor had dropped more than fifty feet, triggering a massive tsunami. It moved at more than four hundred miles per hour in all directions, including the California coast line. The quake and tsunami would prove to be one of the greatest natural disasters to strike southern California.

Alarms sounded all across the new nation, and by 7:47 AM the effects of the quake were being felt all over southern part of the country. Almost immediately, bridges collapsed on every major highway in the Los Angeles area. It was the middle of the morning rush hour, and could not have come at a worse time. Buildings began to sway; although many were designed to withstand earthquakes, the swaying caused windows to break, showering the ground with shards of glass, killing and injuring the pedestrians walking to their jobs.

At 8:09 AM the tsunami struck the Port of Los Angeles with a wave that was more than sixty-five feet high. The power of the wave wasn't diminished by the concrete breakwaters installed to prevent the damage that was about to occur. The mooring lines were no match for the power of the wave. It snapped the lines and tossed the ships about like matchsticks. Every ship was either severely damaged or destroyed. The wave finally dissipated a quarter of a mile inland. Like the ships, every building touched by the moving wall of water was severely damaged or destroyed.

By the time the Earth had stopped shaking, fourteen bridges had collapsed, killing fifty-seven people. More than twenty thousand cars were stranded on the highways, which turned the freeways into massive parking lots.

There were broken water mains all over the city, and electrical power was nonexistent for almost everyone in the southern part of California. Thousands of homes, apartment buildings, offices, and stores had significant structural damage that would take weeks to evaluate, and more than hundred thousand people were left homeless.

President Haskell received a call just before 11:00 AM and was told about the quake and tsunami. She made an immediate decision to call President Peterson. She spoke to his assistant, Ellen Miller. President Haskell told her that the United States was prepared to offer whatever help was needed including medical personnel, food, water, and medicine. Ellen thanked her and said she would inform President Peterson immediately. A few minutes later Ellen called back. She thanked President Haskell for her kind offer, but said President Peterson was not interested in any assistance from the United States.

President Haskell could hardly believe what she was told. She knew Adam Peterson was obstinate, but she never thought he was stupid. There was no way California would recover from this disaster without assistance. She decided to call a press conference and let the world know that California had refused her offer of help.

The news conference was called for 2:30 PM, and the press briefing room was packed. By that time, the scope of the disaster was fairly well known. Initial estimates of damage were in excess of one hundred billion dollars, and many thought the estimate was low. At exactly 2:30 PM President Haskell stepped to the podium and began to speak.

"As all of you are aware, a catastrophic Earthquake and tsunami struck southern California this morning. Although our relationship with California is strained at the moment, I decided to overlook any differences we have. I called President Peterson immediately after I was informed of the disaster and offered to help in any way we could. My offer was rejected without explanation. Despite that rebuke, my offer still stands.

"The United States will provide whatever assistance we can to the people of California in this time of extreme need. All it takes is a phone call. I urge the residents of California to let their government know that this is not the time to act foolishly. At the present time there is no electrical service or fresh water available. We can help by reconnecting California to the United States electrical grid, and we can bring in hundreds of tanker trucks filled with fresh water. We can also supply food, medicine, and medical personnel. Additionally, the Army Corps of Engineers stands ready to assist in rebuilding roads, bridges, and any other tasks that might be required.

"There are no strings attached to this offer. The United States always helps those areas that have been struck by natural disasters, and this is a case where we know help is needed."

Then, pointing her finger at the crowd of reporters, she said, "I'm counting on all of you to get the word out that we are willing and happy to help California. Please don't let me down."

President Haskell left the podium and walked out of the briefing room, ignoring all the questions being asked. Roy Stuart took his place at the podium to answer the questions.

Just before five o'clock, President Haskell was notified that Adam Peterson was on the phone waiting to speak with her.

"President Peterson, I want to extend my sincerest condolences to the people of California. We stand ready to help in any way we can."

"Madam President, since your news conference my office has been deluged with people asking why I rejected your offer of assistance. The reason for my actions is that I didn't want to put California in a position where we would owe a debt to the United States. I still feel that way, but our citizens do not. They want us to accept help from anyone who offers it. So, I find myself in a position where I have to put my own feelings secondary to those of our citizens."

"I really don't understand why you feel that way. When the United States provides assistance to countries that have experienced natural disasters, we never ask for anything in return. Would you refuse help from China?"

"I don't know, but China has not offered any assistance. Canada and Mexico have both offered to help us. I believe it's a question of logistics. China is simply too far away to help in any significant way. At the present time we're still trying to assess the damage. The death toll now stands at two hundred fourteen, and we expect that to rise substantially. The Port of Los Angeles has been completed obliterated. Most of the highways are impassible because of abandoned vehicles and collapsed bridges. Our hospitals were already overcrowded and we are unable to provide care for the people injured by the quake. The most serious problem is lack of water. We need the water mains repaired, and parts of the aqueduct were damaged as well. If you could assist us with the water situation, I would be most grateful."

"I'm not a civil engineer, but I'm sure the Army has people who can help with you with this. I'll have someone call you back shortly to work out the details."

"Thank you. Two of our power generating facilities were damaged, but they have the personnel to resolve those problems. However, we have downed power lines all over the area. Our crews are working on them, but we need additional people for that as well. Finally, would it be possible to have the Navy dispatch a hospital ship to the area to take care of our injured?"

"I'll check on that too."

"Thank you for your help. I'll be waiting for a call."

President Haskell called Roy and told him what she needed. Ten minutes later he called her back. "Madam President, General Bishop, who is in command of the Army Corps of Engineers, is calling President Peterson as we speak. I spoke to Admiral Harris regarding the hospital ship. He said a there's a hospital ship based in San Diego and it can be in Los Angeles by tomorrow evening. It will dock in Long Beach. The port there received only minor damage and is fully operational. Admiral Harris will be contacting President Peterson shortly."

"Thanks Roy, I don't know what I would do without you."

"You're welcome. I'll call President Peterson in an hour or so to make sure everything is okay."

"Please keep me informed if any problems arise."

"Of course."

President Haskell was pleased that California was now willing to accept assistance from the United States, but she was a politician, and she spent the next several minutes wondering how she could use the situation in California to her advantage. She had to find a way to loosen China's grip on California.

XVIII
Sacramento
July 17, 2025

After he ended the call to President Haskell, Adam began to feel a little better about the situation. That feeling would not last for long. As the sun began to set in Los Angeles, the looting began. There was virtually no police presence anywhere in the city. Gangs, some with more than fifty members, began to roam the streets. In many areas every store was robbed of anything even remotely valuable. Store owners, who were not allowed to own guns due to overzealous state gun laws, were unable to protect either themselves or their property. When confronted by the gangs, many simply left the store and allowed the looters unfettered access to the merchandise within. Larger stores that had armed security guards were closed and locked. The guards were posted outside the doors with their guns drawn. Those stores were left unscathed.

By 10:00 PM, almost every drug store in the area was robbed of their entire pharmaceutical inventory.

When California became an independent country, the State Police were renamed the California National Police. As soon as Adam was informed about the looting, he called the Chief of the national police, Thomas Reston, to see what could be done to curb the looting.

"Thomas, I assume you are aware of the situation in Los Angeles. Do you have a plan to stop the looting?"

"No sir, our force is spread over the entire country. We have less than two hundred officers available in the Los Angeles area. They have limited mobility because of the conditions of the roads and the problems with abandoned cars. To be effective, we would need ten times that many people. Also, they would have to be heavily armed and would have to patrol the streets on foot. That would put them in extreme danger."

"Can we call out the National Guard?"

"Sir, during his first week in office, President Nelson disbanded the national guard. I am unsure of his reasoning and I advised him against doing it, but he ignored me."

With extreme disgust in his voice, Adam Peterson replied, "Isn't that wonderful. So, we have no way of dealing with the situation, is that correct?"

"Sir, I can move all of my officers from the northern part of the country to Los Angeles, but that will take time. They can begin to patrol the area tomorrow evening. However, they have neither the training or the weapons needed for that type of duty."

Adam thought for a moment and said, "I can't do anything about the training, but the National Guard weapons have to be somewhere. Bring as many officers as you can to the Los Angeles area as quickly as possible. I'll see what we can do about getting them adequate weapons."

"Yes, sir. I think I can probably get another two thousand officers there by tomorrow afternoon. I'll send out the orders immediately."

"Thank you, Thomas."

Adam called his assistant, Ellen, and said, "I'm sorry to bother you this late, but the situation in Los Angeles is critical. I'm sure you're aware of the looting."

"Yes sir, I've been watching the news. Apparently, a gang of about thirty-five looters tried to rob one of the Advanced Electronics Outlet stores. There were ten guards outside the building guarding the entrance. The gang ignored the order to disband from the guard in charge. Then someone from the group shot at the guard. The shot missed, but the guards opened fire on the mob, killing seven and wounding another five. The uninjured looters left immediately."

Adam yelled, "Shit! What do I do now? I just discovered that Nelson disbanded the national guard. Did you know that?"

"No sir, I didn't. Why would he do that?"

"I have no idea, and neither did Thomas Reston. I think we have to write off tonight, but by tomorrow Thomas said he would order two thousand of his officers available to patrol the Los Angeles area. However, they need the weapons the National Guard had. I don't care who you have to wake up, I need you to find those weapons tonight."

"Yes sir, I'll take care of it."

The California Experiment

At 4:00 AM more than two thousand members of the Army Corps of Engineers crossed into California in a truck convoy over a mile long. Their destination was the empty Air Force base in El Segundo. That was also the destination for the officers of the California National Police who had been ordered to the Los Angeles area. They were followed by a convoy of tanker trucks carrying fresh water.

About the same time the Army personnel arrived in California, Ellen had succeeded in locating the weapons that were previously the property of the California National Guard. They were located in a storage facility in Bakersfield. She contacted Thomas Reston and told him where the weapons were. He said he would get some helicopters to transfer the weapons to the El Segundo base.

As the sun rose over Los Angeles, the level of destruction caused by the previous night's looting became obvious. Helicopters from various news agencies were sending live pictures of the devastation all over the world. In some areas of Los Angeles, virtually every store was looted. Drug stores, hardware stores, electronics stores, and grocery stores were especially hard hit.

At 7:39 AM, the first of several aftershocks shook the area again. The first, and strongest, registered 6.9 on the Richter Scale. It was centered only a few miles southeast from the center of the original quake. Three more aftershocks followed in the next twenty minutes. They were all less powerful and only registered about 5.0. The quakes caused little additional damage, but the residents of the area, unable to drive because of road conditions, began to flee the area on foot. Most were more concerned about the gangs that now owned the streets than they were about the quakes.

President Peterson was watching the events unfold on the television in his office. As he watched, it quickly became obvious he would have to declare martial law. He issued the order at 8:15 AM, and contacted Thomas Reston to inform him. Thomas thanked him and said that would make his job a little easier.

The weapons had arrived at the El Segundo base, and the helicopters used to transport the weapons were now used to transport police squads to the areas currently controlled by street gangs. They were armed with tear gas grenades, and most of the weapons were loaded with non-lethal bullets. The idea was to break up the gangs, not kill them. But they were ordered to use lethal force if they deemed it necessary.

The first job for the Army was to repair the broken water mains, and by 9:30 AM helicopters began to take repair teams and their equipment to the six known water main breaks. Each team included four guards who were responsible for the safety of their teams.

Teams were also dispatched to repair downed power lines, and by 12:30 PM some power had been restored. President Peterson thought things were beginning to look a little better, and he called President Haskell to thank her for the help.

Most cell phone service was restored by 4:00 PM. As soon as that happened an emergency message was sent to inform the public that martial law was in force and there was a dusk curfew. Anyone found on the streets after dusk was subject to arrest. Unfortunately, for many there was no place to go. So, as night approached, the police ignored small groups who were obviously not posing any danger. They concentrated on looking for gangs. As the sun set, they appeared again, although there were fewer targets to hit. But the police were prepared. During the next few hours there were several confrontations between the street gangs and the police. However, the police were able to disperse the gangs without the use of deadly force.

The following morning it was obvious some sense of order had been restored, and many of the people who left the day before began to return to their homes. However, many didn't have much of a home to return to.

Right after California became an independent country, insurance companies based in the remaining states sent letters to the policyholders in California informing them they were unable to continue servicing their policies, the balance of their premiums would be returned, and they would have to find insurance from another company. However, a majority of the policyholders either didn't understand or simply ignored the letters. But the policy refund checks were cashed. Now that cell phone service had been restored, they began to call their insurance companies to file claims. Most became enraged when they were told that their policies were no longer in force and they contacted the government to inform them of the dilemma.

President Peterson was aware of the situation because his company, and his home, were both insured with a company based in New York. So, his staff switched to a company based in California. Apparently, most of residents of Los Angeles ignored the letters and they were expecting the government to pay to have their homes repaired and personal property replaced. He glanced down at a paper on his desk. It said the death toll had risen to four hundred and eight, and damage was estimated at about a half trillion dollars. There was no way he could help.

The Navy hospital ship, The Helping Hand, arrived a day later than expected because some of the medical staff were on leave. But when it arrived in Long Beach, it was fully staffed and the staff was eager to help anyone who needed it. When the port was visible, the captain contacted the Los Angeles County Health Department and informed them that in about forty-five minutes they would be able to accept patients.

Because of road conditions, most patients were brought in by helicopter. The ship had three landings pads, and they were kept constantly busy for the next five hours. Patients also arrived on foot, and several motorcycles with side cars began bringing patients as well. Ten hours after the Helping Hand docked, they had treated two hundred eighty-one patients. Most of them were treated and released because they had relatively minor injuries, but emergency surgery was needed for fifty-one people. There were several with a severe head trauma, many with broken legs and arms, and a few with back injuries.

Throughout the night, new patients continued to arrive, and by morning there were more than a hundred people waiting for treatment. As they began to treat the waiting patients, they found that more than half were new immigrants who were ill but uninjured in the quake. They didn't turn anyone away, but the captain was concerned because they came there to treat the injured from the quake. Now, many of the people who asked for treatment had communicable diseases, and they were a threat to the injured patients who had weakened immune systems. He made the decision to set up a triage area at the entrance of the ship. Patients who were ill, but uninjured, were treated in the triage area and wouldn't be allowed to board. He contacted the County Health Department notifying them of this procedure. He was immediately told that he could not discriminate between patients, and all patients had to be treated equally. The captain told the person at the health department in no uncertain terms that he was in command of the ship, and would do what he felt was best for his patients. Then he said that if they want all the patients treated equally, just bring in the injured, not the sick, and he ended the call.

Two hours later two large tents were set up. One for triage and one for the treatment of patients who were ill, but uninjured. This allowed the staff to care for the patients much faster, and as a result the line quickly dwindled to a point where there were only a few people waiting to be seen.

Both President Peterson and Ellen arrived at the Capitol before 7:00 AM. They sat down together at a table in Adam's office, each drinking a cup of coffee. After exchanging pleasantries for a few minutes Ellen said, "I spent several hours researching the number of the home owners whose homes were damaged in the quake and had no insurance. The number is much higher than I expected. It would appear that almost forty percent failed to purchase new insurance when their old policies were cancelled. How are we going to handle this?"

"I don't think California should be responsible for the actions of people who were stupid enough to allow their insurance to lapse. The letters were very clear, and when they received refund checks it should have been obvious that they needed to find insurance elsewhere. I'm positive they also received notices from their mortgage lenders. I think the only thing we could do would be to make low interest loans available to those who need it. See if you can get an estimate of how much would be needed."

"I can do that, but we also have to consider that many of these people are going to be out of work for a while. That probably means no payments for at least three months. I suspect we don't have enough in the treasury to make the loans. I'll discuss it with the treasurer as soon as I get some idea of how much we need."

"Okay, keep me informed. Also, set up a news conference for this evening so I can let our people know the status of the repair efforts."

"Yes, sir."

The camera crews were set up in President Peterson's office. At exactly 7:00 PM he began to speak.

"Good evening, I wanted to bring all of our citizens up to date on the status of the repair efforts in the Los Angeles area. So, I will begin with the good news. The United States has sent in more than two thousand members of the Army Corps of Engineers. Working with maintenance personnel for Los Angeles County, and other neighboring counties, we have managed to restore electrical power to ninety percent of the buildings. Cell phone service has already been restored. All of the water mains have been repaired, and temporary repairs have been made to the aqueduct. As a result, most homes and businesses have fresh water again. However, the department of health recommends that water be boiled before drinking it for the next few days. Also, we have fifty-four fresh water stations set up in the area. They are giving free gallon bottles of purified drinking water to anyone who asks. To find the location of your nearest water station, please check the government website. I'm also pleased to inform you that the United States Navy sent a hospital ship to Long Beach, and they have been providing care for those injured in the quake. Perhaps the best news of all is that our geologists have told us that it is unlikely there would be any additional powerful aftershocks.

"Unfortunately, the death toll from the quake now stands at five hundred eighty-three, making it one of the deadliest quakes in California history, second only to the San Francisco quake in 1906. We have crews working around the clock on infrastructure repairs, but we have to rebuild or repair more than twenty bridges before we can reopen the freeways. With the help we are receiving from the United States Army, we hope to complete that task in the next fifteen days. Many of the repairs will be temporary, but the freeways will be useable again. Because of the nature of the repairs, most heavy trucks will not be allowed to use them until permanent repairs are completed, and that could take up to a year.

"Many of our school buildings have been damaged and they are being evaluated by our engineers. So far, they have only found three schools that have major damage. However, since schools are closed for the summer, there is sufficient time to complete the repairs before the classes resume.

"Lastly, I have been informed that many of the homeowners in the area hit by the quake allowed their homeowners insurance to lapse and are apparently expecting the government to pay for the repairs to their homes. I'm sorry to inform you that we are unable to do that. We're looking into the possibility of setting up a low interest loan program to pay for needed repairs. The damage caused by the quake is now estimated at almost a half-trillion dollars, and we have to pay for infrastructure repairs first.

"Thank you for your time this evening. I will be speaking to you again soon. Goodnight."

Early the next morning, President Peterson's office received a call from the Chinese Ambassador requesting an appointment with the president as soon as possible. The meeting was set up for 1:00 o'clock that afternoon.

The Chinese Ambassador arrived a few minutes early, and Ellen brought him into President Peterson's office. After exchanging greetings, the Ambassador sat down across from the president and said, "I saw your speech last night and have been instructed by my government to offer our help with the current situation. We know California does not have sufficient funds to deal with the problems created by the earthquake. We are prepared to loan California three hundred billion dollars, which should be more than sufficient to fund all the necessary repairs. Additionally, there is zero interest on the loan, and the terms of the loan will not require any cash repayment. Instead, we would like to lease some properties in California that are currently owned by the government. The lease payments would be deducted from the principal balance."

President Peterson was surprised by the offer, and he knew California certainly needed the money, but he also knew the Chinese aren't in the habit of making interest free loans. He thought about it for a few seconds and then asked, "What properties are you interested in?"

"The properties we are interested in are the 29 Palms Marine Base and Edwards Air Force Base."

"What is your plan for the properties?"

"We would like to use Edwards as a military base and convert 29 Palms into a residential development. If California accepts our proposal, we will work with you to make sure you find our plans acceptable."

"What are the terms of the lease?"

"The lease term would be one hundred years. Each year reduces the loan principle by three billion dollars. Both of these areas would be tax-free zones. No sales, income, or property taxes."

"Mr. Ambassador, I do not have the authority to accept or reject such an offer. It would have to be approved by the California legislature. That being said, I find your offer interesting. Please put it writing and I'll submit it to our finance committee for review."

The Chinese Ambassador opened his briefcase, removed a file folder, and handed it to President Peterson. Then he said, "I believe this is what you will need to fully evaluate our offer. We would like an answer in ten days, if that is possible."

"Thank you, Mr. Ambassador. I'll do my best to meet your time frame."

"You're welcome, Mr. President. Please do not hesitate to contact me if you have any questions."

"Of course."

As soon as the ambassador left his office, Adam called Ellen and said, "Ellen, please get me any information you can find regarding Edwards Air Force Base and the 29 Palms Marine base."

"May I ask why?"

"The Chinese want to lease them in exchange for giving us three hundred billion dollars."

"Wow! That would get us out of the financial mess we're in. Did they tell you why they wanted them?"

"Not exactly."

"It won't take me long to get the information you need."

"Thanks Ellen."

An hour later Ellen called Adam and said, "I have some information for you. Edwards Air Force Base is about twenty-two square miles in size. It was one of the primary sites for missile testing. It was also supposed to be used for launching rockets for space exploration, but it was never actually used for that purpose. Prior to the United States abandoning the base, there were about three thousand five hundred active military personnel stationed there. All of the launch facilities and associated equipment was destroyed before the base was abandoned. However, the housing units were left undamaged.

"29 Palms is enormous, about 998 square miles, which is bigger than a lot of countries. It had about nine thousand five hundred military personnel prior to being abandoned. It was primarily used by the Marines as a training center. The United States left most of the base untouched when they left."

"Thanks for the information Ellen. It seems to me with that much space we could easily find ourselves with a million or more Chinese people in the middle of our country. I'm not sure I like that."

"Have you thought about the possibility of having a million or more Chinese soldiers in the middle of our country? That's what scares me."

"The ambassador said they wanted to use Edwards as a military base, and 29 Palms as a residential development. But, of course, that doesn't mean the residents can't be soldiers. It's not my decision. The legislature will have to decide."

Adam called Jean Foreman, the chairperson of the senate finance committee, and asked her to come by his office as soon as possible. She said she would be there at 3:00 PM.

Adam and Jean had been friends for years, and she was one of the few women Adam had ever dated on a regular basis. When she arrived at his office they hugged briefly and Adam asked her to sit down. He said, "Jean, it's nice to see you again. It's been a while since we went out together. Would you like to go to dinner this evening?"

"Of course, Adam. I'd like that very much, but you could have asked me to dinner when we spoke on the phone."

"I guess I've been so busy with everything that's going on I didn't realize how much I missed you until you got here. Anyway, the reason I asked you to come here is because I wanted to give you this." Then he handed her the file folder he received from the Chinese Ambassador.

Jean opened the file and read the contents for a few minutes. Then she looked up at Adam and said, "I know we need the money desperately, but I'm not sure this is the solution."

"I agree completely, but I think the entire finance committee should review the proposal before we make any decisions. The Chinese want an answer in ten days."

"I'll call a meeting for tomorrow morning."

"Thanks, I'll pick you up at 7:00 PM. Is that okay?"

"Perfect, I'll see you later."

After Jean left, Adam asked his secretary to contact President Haskell. Five minutes later he was speaking with her.

"Good afternoon, Madam President. I wanted to call you to thank you personally for the assistance the United States has provided. We're making great progress in repairing the damage caused by the quake."

"You're welcome. We're happy to help. I saw your speech last night. I must tell you that I didn't realize the extent of the damage until then."

"The damage was extensive, and we aren't currently in a position to fund all the repairs that need to be done. This morning I received a visit from the Chinese Ambassador. They offered to give us the money needed to pay for the repairs in exchange for a one-hundred-year lease on Edwards Air Force Base and the 29 Palms Marine Base."

"I hope you aren't seriously considering accepting their offer."

"The decision isn't mine. I have given it to our senate finance committee for evaluation. If the finance committee approves the proposal, it will have to be voted on by the entire legislature."

"Do you realize they could easily have in excess of a million soldiers based at 29 Palms? They could take over California in a heartbeat."

"Believe me, Madam President, I'm fully aware of the possible consequences of having that many Chinese soldiers in California. The ambassador said they wanted Edwards as a military base and 29 Palms for a residential development."

"I'm not sure about the size, but I believe 29 Palms is hundreds of square miles. That would be more than a little excessive as a housing project."

"Actually, 29 Palms is nine hundred ninety-eight square miles. It's mostly high desert, and not a very good area for residential development. There is very little water, and only a few roads. Other than the area that was built for the base, it's mostly barren. So I agree, they probably aren't planning a residential development. But, it's not a great area for a large military base either. They would have to spend billions of dollars to make it suitable for any kind of development."

"I urge you not to accept their proposal. I'm sure you can veto any measure passed by your legislature, and if it passes, you should do that."

"I will consider your advice. I wanted to make you aware of the situation. Thank you for your time, Madam President."

"You're welcome."

President Peterson's limo pulled up in front of Jean's house at 7:00 o'clock. She was waiting on her front porch. The limo driver opened the door for her and she sat down next to Adam in the back seat. She kissed him lightly on the cheek. Then she said, "I read through the entire file you gave me. Did you read it completely?"

"No, I only read the synopsis on the first page. I didn't get into the detail."

"Then you probably don't know there were some things that would have to be done before we would receive the money."

"Such as?"

"There were two items I was concerned about. They want us to end our trading relationship with Taiwan, and they want us to close our open border with Mexico. They feel there must be some set of conditions that have to be met before people can enter California."

Adam could not believe what he heard. He was visibly shaken, and stuttered slightly when he asked, "Did they say why they wanted us to restrict access through our border with Mexico?"

"Surprisingly, they did. They said the economic viability of California will be substantially diminished by the uncontrolled influx of immigrants from Mexico and Central America. They're planning on investing billions of dollars to develop these two properties, and they are concerned their investments might be wasted."

Adam realized immediately that there was some truth in the Chinese statement. Still, he was sure the people of California wanted open borders, regardless of the consequences. However, the decision was now in the hands of the finance committee. He asked Jean, "How do you feel about their proposal?"

"On the surface it appears to be a great idea, but I have no desire to close the border with Mexico, and I'm concerned about having a large number of Chinese people, and probably soldiers, in California. It could be the first step in allowing China to get a foothold in North America. We have no army or any way to defend ourselves. They could easily take over our country without firing a shot."

"Those are my thoughts as well. If we get through the current crisis, become financially stable, and have a growing economy, we become ripe for takeover. On the other hand, if the current crisis becomes too much for us to handle and we find ourselves in financial trouble, they probably wouldn't want us."

Jean was silent for a moment. Then she looked at Adam and said, "I'm sorry to disagree with you Adam, but the more I think about this, the more I believe they would want us either way."

"What if we took some action to make us less of an easy target? Supposing we accept their offer, but use some of the money to build an army. That might keep them in check."

"That's an interesting idea, and you've given me one too." She took a breath and continued, "Supposing we require all immigrants who meet some specific conditions to serve in our army in order to become citizens of California? That might meet the

Chinese requirement for restricted access, and at the same time, allow us to build an army."

Adam laughed and said, "Do you really think the Chinese are going to help us build an army to protect us from them?"

"Okay, so instead of having them join our future army, how about if we have them work on infrastructure projects. They actually become employees of California. Then, if it looks like there's going to be a conflict, we draft them."

Adam thought about what Jean said. He replied, "I think that's a great idea. Let's get the legislature to pass a law that requires everyone employed by California to be subject to conscription into the California Community Corps if there's an emergency."

Jean looked puzzled and asked, "What's the California Community Corps?"

"It's our army."

"Won't the Chinese realize that?"

"They probably won't make the connection, at least not immediately. The immigrants will receive the training required to perform community services. Nothing that overtly looks like combat training. I don't think the Chinese will become suspicious."

"I'm confused. What good is an untrained army? I don't think we'll ever be able to match the Chinese in numbers, so how will they be able to protect us?"

"I think you may be wrong about the numbers. Until the quake stuck, we were getting about fifteen hundred immigrants per day. Right now, only about a hundred per day are coming, but that number will increase rapidly as things get back to normal. At least a third of them are potential conscripts. That's a few thousand per month."

"If you are going to require them to join our army in order to get across the border, it will probably reduce that number substantially."

"We're not requiring them to join our army. Remember, we are going to give them community service jobs. I think the promise of a job may actually increase the number of people who will want to come here. They only have the potential of being drafted into our army if there is an emergency. Also, I'm sure we can include some weapons and self-defense training as part of their community service training so they won't be totally untrained.

Jean sighed deeply, "Well, we can try. I'll discuss it with the committee tomorrow. But if we make this deal with the Chinese, won't the United States pull out all of their people who are helping us with the repairs?"

"Probably, but I think they'll be gone in five or six weeks anyway. I'm sure we can keep the arrangement secret for that long."

Jean met with the finance committee the next morning, and after a couple of hours of discussion, they agreed to recommend the legislature accept the Chinese offer. They also agreed to introduce a bill the next day to create the California Community Corps, and included in the bill was a requirement that everyone who worked for California was subject to conscription if the government declared an emergency. There was also sufficient funding to have five thousand permanent members of the corps.

Jean called Adam and told him what the committee had done. He was very pleased, and he told her now they would have to draft legislation that would provide funding for immigrants to work on community service projects. She said she would take care of it.

Then Adam called Ellen and asked her to set up a meeting with the Chinese Ambassador for the following day.

The meeting was arranged for 11:00 o'clock and the ambassador arrived at Adam's office a few minutes early. Adam's secretary brought him into the office immediately. Adam stood up, and smiling said, "Good morning, Mr. Ambassador. Thank you for coming on such short notice. Would you like some coffee or tea?"

"Some tea would be very nice, thank you, Mr. President."

Looking at his secretary Adam said, "Please bring in some tea and coffee."

Adam and the Chinese Ambassador sat down at the table in his office. Adam said, "Mr. Ambassador, our finance committee has recommended the legislature accept your most generous offer. I want to discuss the actions you required California to take as part of the agreement. We are not currently purchasing any products directly from Taiwan, so that is not an issue. However, there may be a problem with restricting entry into California from Mexico. I'm sure you realize that one of the reasons we seceded from the United States was because we felt United States immigration regulations were harsh and inhumane. What we are prepared to do is require that all adults who want to enter California on a permanent basis must either have fifty thousand dollars in liquid assets, a job, or agree to work for California performing community service projects. Would that be acceptable?"

"I'm not the one who makes the decisions, but I believe our government will probably find that satisfactory. Has your legislature approved your plan?"

"That will happen in the next few days. Actually, all they have to approve is the funding for the community service work. I already have the authority to alter immigration rules. So, the new rules will be implemented as soon as the funds are allocated. That will happen regardless of the decision made by your government regarding the loan."

"I'm happy to hear that. Have you considered what will happen with the aid you are receiving from the United States if the loan is approved? I know President Haskell will be very displeased with your decision."

"I am hoping we can delay any public announcement for five or six weeks. By that time, the tasks the United States Army is working on should be completed."

"I believe we can do that, but I will contact my government and make certain."

"I would like to know what the plans are for the areas China will be leasing."

"I know the plan for Edwards is to become a military base. There will be a full Air Force Squadron based there. There will also be a few hundred civilian employees and perhaps five hundred soldiers. Most of the civilians employed at the base will be people who live in the area. I haven't seen any plans for the 29 Palms area, but I know it will be residential, not military. We will keep you informed as our plans become more finalized."

"Thank you, I appreciate that. I can understand why Edwards would be useful, but the 29 Palms area is high desert. There's almost no water and the summertime temperatures are almost unbearable. China would have to spend billions to make the area habitable."

"As I said, I don't know the plans for the area. I'm sure the people who made the request for 29 Palms are familiar with the area, and I trust they know what they are doing. You should do the same."

"Of course."

A few minutes later, the ambassador left. Adam was sure the ambassador was hiding something, but he had no idea what.

Russell Fine

XIX
The Oval Office
July 24, 2025

Roy Stuart knocked lightly on the door to the Oval Office, then opened the door. President Haskell looked up from what she was reading and said, "Good morning Roy, what's up?"

"I have some very disturbing news from California and I've confirmed the information is correct."

"Do I really want to hear this?"

"Probably not, but you have to. I suspect it'll make you angry, but try to control yourself."

"You're scaring me. Okay, just spit it out and I promise not to kill the messenger."

"Thanks," Roy sighed deeply and continued, "China has offered to loan California three hundred billion dollars to pay for the repairs after the quake. They want to be repaid by leasing Edwards and 29 Palms at no charge for a hundred years. California agreed to the terms and the measure was passed by their legislature yesterday."

President Haskell was silent for almost a minute. Then she said, "That son-of-a-bitch Peterson is going to be sorry he did this. Pull our Army personnel immediately. I want them all out of California in twenty-four hours."

"I was sure you were going to say that. What about their water supply? Do you want to cut that off too?"

"Not yet, that's my trump card. I want to save that for the proper time."

"You may be pleased to know there are now restrictions for becoming a citizen of California. Apparently, it was part of the agreement with China. All adults must have fifty thousand dollars in liquid assets, a job, or agree to work for the government."

"Well, they finally did something logical instead of emotional. Do we know what China plans to do with the property they're leasing?"

"They're going to put an Air Force squadron at Edwards, but nobody knows their plans for 29 Palms."

With a note of sarcasm in her voice, President Haskell said, "Isn't that just perfect! Anyway, get our people out of there as soon as possible. I don't want President Peterson to know why the Army is leaving yet."

"I understand. I'll take care of it immediately."

By that evening, the United States Army personnel who were helping with the quake damage began to leave California. None of them knew why they were leaving, and when questioned about it they couldn't respond other than saying, "We don't know."

It didn't take long for Adam to find out the United States Army was leaving before the job was finished. He should have realized the United States had spies in the legislature, but he was, none the less, very disappointed. Now the work would take longer to complete, and California would have to pay for the repairs. He was wondering if he should call President Haskell and ask why the Army was leaving, even though he already knew the answer. Additionally, he was worried she would order the water supply to be cut off, and he hoped she wouldn't take that action. Ultimately, he decided to call her the next morning.

The following morning, President Haskell was told that President Peterson was on the phone. She answered by saying cheerfully, "Good morning, President Peterson, how are things going?"

"Good morning, Madam President. May I ask why you ordered your Army personnel out of California? I thought they would stay until their work was completed."

"Please don't act naïve, you know why I pulled the United States troops out. I think you should ask your new best friends for help."

"Obviously you have been informed about our agreement with China. I had little choice. California didn't have the necessary resources to complete the infrastructure repairs needed after the quake. I must ask you to please not take any action to cut off the water supply to southern California."

"I won't at this time. I realize that California has some current financial problems, but since you will soon be getting a substantial infusion of cash, I may ask you to begin paying for the water you are using at some future time."

"I suppose that would be reasonable."

"I can understand why the Chinese wants Edwards, but what on Earth could they do with 29 Palms?"

"I've asked them that same question. All they will tell me is that it will be a residential development."

"Have you considered the possibility that this may be the first step in a plan to take over California?"

"Of course I have, and so has the legislature. They believe the risk is minimal, and that's why they approved the agreement."

"Do you believe the risk is minimal as well?"

"No, I don't. But I don't believe the risk is substantial either. We're taking steps to create a military force, but I don't think for a minute we would be able to stop them if they invaded us."

"I'm positive they wouldn't invade California if they could take control through financial rather than military means. I would advise you to be prepared."

"You think they're going to buy us?"

"Yes, I do, and they have already started the process."

"Well, you've given me something to think about, Madam President. Thank you for taking the time to speak to me."

"You're welcome."

As she hung up the phone, she had a horrible thought. She picked up her phone again and called Roy. She asked him to come to her office immediately.

Roy knocked lightly and opened the door. President Haskell said, "Please sit down, Roy. I have a task I need performed immediately, and it's confidential. Nobody, except the people working on the project, can know anything about it."

"Of course, Madam President."

"I just finished speaking with President Peterson. When the conversation was over, I had an idea, and I want you to check it out. Basically, what I want to know is this; is it possible that the Earthquake which struck Los Angeles was manmade?"

Roy was so surprised by the request he was unable to speak for a few moments. Then he said, "Do you realize the implications of what you're asking? I assume you think the Chinese are responsible. If that proves to be the case, it's an act of war."

"That's why this must be kept confidential. If there's proof, I will confront the Chinese Ambassador with the information and watch him squirm."

"I'll contact the United States Geological Survey immediately."

"No, contact the Secretary of the Interior, Gwen Forester. They report to her. Make sure she understands this is absolutely top secret. If I hear about this on TV or read about it in the paper, there will be some personnel changes here," she said emphatically.

"Got it."

"Thanks, Roy."

XX
The Oval Office
July 31, 2025

President Haskell was in her office when the secretary knocked on the door. She opened the door slightly and said, "Madam President, Gwen Forester is here. She would like to speak with you."

"Please send her in."

Gwen Forester walked into the Oval Office. She looked around for a few moments before President Haskell spoke, "Good morning Gwen. Please sit down."

"Thank you, Madam President. Please forgive me, but I've never been in the Oval Office before."

"I didn't realize that. I guess all our meetings have been in one of the conference rooms. Anyway, what brings you here today?"

"We finished our initial analysis of the Earthquake you requested. The quake occurred on a minor fault line. Our geologists were very surprised at the magnitude of the quake when it occurred, but they didn't consider the possibility that it may have been manmade. After researching the quake, they believe there's a strong possibility the quake may have been triggered by a powerful explosion that preceded the quake by forty seconds. The explosion was recorded on instruments all around the Pacific rim. The other thing we were able to learn was the explosion occurred on the sea floor. In that area, the ocean is about nineteen hundred feet deep. In order to generate a quake like that one, the explosive would have to be set in a very precise location. There's no way to do that without a deep-water submersible or a submarine, and there are a very limited number of countries with that capability."

So, President Haskell's fear that the quake was an act of war had been confirmed. It was not what she wanted to hear. She asked, "Are you absolutely positive the quake was intentionally triggered?"

"No, I can't be absolutely sure, but all of the geologists who analyzed the data said that a quake of that magnitude was so unlikely to occur on a minor fault line that it had to be caused by some external stimulus."

"Okay, thank you for the information. As I'm sure you are aware, this information is confidential. Do not discuss this with anyone, and please make sure the geologists who worked on the report understand how important it is that this information remain secret for the time being."

"Yes, Madam President. I've already informed them about that. They will not discuss it with anyone. I didn't want to write a report, which is why I wanted to give the information to you in person."

"Thank you, Gwen. I really appreciate it."

As soon as Gwen left, President Haskell summoned Roy again. When he arrived, she said, "Roy, we now have confirmation that the quake was manmade. I need to know if we have satellite images of the area where the quake occurred for two or three weeks prior to the quake. I have to know if there were any ships in the area. Again, this is confidential."

"Yes, I know that. This is really bad news for California. Are you going to tell them?"

"I'm not sure yet. I may want to discuss it with the Chinese first. In any event, we need verification that there were Chinese ships in the area prior to the quake."

"I'll get right on it."

"Thanks."

It didn't take long for Roy to find out that a Chinese container ship stopped in the area of the fault line for almost forty-eight hours ten days before the quake occurred. The ship reported electrical problems, and it arrived at its destination two days late. Roy immediately informed President Haskell. It was exactly what she suspected. It was almost six o'clock, but still early afternoon in California. She asked her secretary to call President Peterson immediately.

Ten minutes later, President Peterson was on the phone and waiting for her. She said, "Good afternoon, President Peterson. I have some interesting news for you."

"Madam President, I'm a very informal guy. Could we do away with the formal titles? Can I call you Nancy, and you can call me Adam?"

"Sure, it does make conversation easier. Adam, I became suspicious regarding the willingness of the Chinese to basically give California three hundred billion dollars. It seemed to be part of a much larger plan. So, my first thought was that perhaps the Chinese had something to do with the Earthquake. I asked our government geologists to investigate the quake more fully, and they discovered there was a very large explosion on the fault line forty seconds before the quake occurred. The explosion was detected by seismographs all around the Pacific."

Adam interrupted her, "Are you telling me the Chinese caused the quake?"

"Yes Adam, that's exactly what I am telling you. Our geologists said the sea floor is very deep there and the explosive had to be placed very precisely. The only way to do it was with a submarine or a deep-water submersible. We also found out that a Chinese container ship stopped in the area for two days, ten days before the quake."

Adam could hardly believe what he was just told. It was too late to terminate the agreement with China. The money had already been transferred to the California treasury, and the Chinese had dispatched personnel to both Edwards and 29 Palms. His voice quivered slightly when he asked, "Are you sure this information is accurate?"

"Yes Adam, I'm sure. But you don't have to take my word for it. Have your own people check the validity of the information."

"I will do that immediately. But I have no idea what action I could take at this point. This was an act of war, but we have no military. Hell, we don't even have a national guard anymore."

"I understand completely. Would you like me to inform the Chinese that we know they caused the quake?"

"I don't see what good that would do. We'll have to figure out what to do on our own. Thank you for letting me know. Goodbye, Nancy."

"Goodbye, Adam."

Russell Fine

XXI
Sacramento, California
August 9, 2025

After Adam hung up the phone, he called Ellen and asked her to come to his office. She came immediately. As soon as she walked in, she could tell by the expression on Adam's face that something was wrong. "You look like your best friend just died. What's going on?"

"I just spoke to President Haskell. She told me the Chinese caused the quake."

"Shit! I hope you're kidding me!"

"I'm not. I'm sure we must have a geologist or two on the California payroll. Contact them and ask them to check out the possibility that a massive explosion occurred on the fault line just before the quake."

Ellen replied, "Yes, of course," and she left Adam's office.

Adam had little doubt the information was correct, but he had no idea what he could do about it. Since California had become independent, the problems had been constant, but until the quake, they were relatively minor. However, this was not a minor problem. He was sure China's plan was to take over the country, and California was powerless to stop it.

Two hours later Ellen came back to Adam's office. She slumped into the chair across from Adams desk, then said, "The geologists at UCLA were already aware of the explosion prior to the quake because they were asked to review the data they had from the quake by the United States Department of the Interior. They didn't connect it to China, and felt it could possibly have been a natural occurrence."

"Do they still feel it could have been a natural occurrence?" Adam asked hopefully.

"No, they don't. They think a manmade explosion is much more likely."

"It would have been so much easier to handle if the quake had been a natural event. This is definitely going to affect how I deal with the Chinese ambassador in the future. Okay, set up a senior staff meeting for tomorrow morning. I don't suppose you asked the geologists to keep this confidential, did you?"

"Actually, I did. They promised not to say anything about it until the information becomes public knowledge."

At 10:00 o'clock the next morning, the leaders of the California Legislature and the leaders of all the cabinet level agencies were gathered in the main conference room in the capitol building. Adam walked in a few minutes later. He received a standing ovation as he walked up to the podium. He motioned for everyone to be seated. Then he began to speak, "Good morning. Thank you for that wonderful welcome. Since we declared our independence, we have had to deal with far more problems than we anticipated. Of course, it was impossible to know that Los Angeles would be devastated by an Earthquake. Until now, we have found ways to deal with our problems effectively. When we were faced with severe financial problems, China stepped in and offered much needed aid."

Adam paused and looked at his audience for a few seconds before he continued, "Or so we thought. The reason for this meeting is to inform you that China, pardon my language, screwed us. I have irrefutable proof that China was responsible for the quake. We owe a debt of gratitude to President Haskell. She became suspicious about the origin of the quake and asked her people to review the data from it to determine if it could have been manmade. Upon a closer review of the data, it was discovered that a massive explosion occurred forty seconds before the quake. It was also discovered that a Chinese container ship stopped over the fault line for two days, ten days prior to prior to the quake. Both the United States and our scientists believe they used a deep-water submersible to position the explosive on the fault line."

Suddenly loud conversations broke out in the crowd. Adam motioned for them to be quiet. When silence returned, he continued.

"We all know the quake was catastrophic, in both the loss of human life and property damage. This was an act of war, and now, with open arms, we have invited our enemy into our country. There can be little doubt their ultimate goal is to take control of California.

We have no military to defend ourselves, and when the time comes, we will be forced to surrender.

"Obviously, this wasn't the goal we expected when we gained our independence. I want you to think about this. If anyone has a possible solution to the problem, please speak up."

Everyone in the audience was stunned by what they just heard. For perhaps a full minute nobody said anything. Then someone asked, "Since President Haskell is aware of the situation, and I'm sure she doesn't want China to take over California, would she consider using the United States military to protect us?"

Adam replied, "I suspect not. We severed our ties with the United States, and we tried to take financial advantage of them. In hindsight, that was a foolish plan, and now we are stuck with the consequences of our own actions."

"We have already started to form an army. Perhaps we will have enough time to complete the task. Then, at least, we could put up a fight."

"That would cause the death of countless California citizens, and it's a fight we could not possibly win. China's military has more than three million people in it. We might be able to muster two hundred thousand, at the most. Also, we don't have the weapons needed to fight a war with China. We need a non-military solution," Adam replied.

Since nobody said anything for a while, Adam concluded the meeting, "Please do not discuss this information with anyone outside this room. Not even your spouses. This must not become public. If anyone comes up with an idea, contact me immediately. Thank you."

Adam left the conference room and went back to his office. He had to come up with a plan.

Now that California was flush with cash, the repairs from the quake were progressing rapidly. Low cost loans were made available to the homeowners who had no insurance, and although it required some prodding from the government, almost every home was insured again.

By the end of September, the Chinese base at Edwards was fully staffed. There were about one hundred planes, their crews, and support staff working at the base. There were also almost a thousand members of the Chinese Army stationed there. In total, Edwards had more than three thousand inhabitants.

Work was also started on 29 Palms. They had begun the construction of a large nuclear power plant, much to the dismay of the nearby population. They also began drilling wells for water, the construction of a large wastewater facility, and laying out more than a hundred miles of roads. All of the work was being done by Chinese crews, although they did purchase the needed building materials locally.

The work on San Onofre was also going well, and they expected the facility to be fully operational by the end of the year. The enhancements at Diablo Canyon were scheduled for completion at almost the same time.

Harold Becker and Roy Stuart spoke almost every week. Harold was probably the only person in California, outside of the government, who knew that the Chinese were responsible for the quake. Harold was anxious to do something, but Roy assured him that he would have a project for him soon, and this time the Chinese would be the target.

The new immigration rules had almost no effect on the number of people asking for permanent residence in California. They were still arriving at the rate of about fifteen thousand per month. Less than ten percent of the able-bodied adults had jobs waiting for them. The rest were assigned to crews that were performing quake repairs.

Most of the new residents were provided housing at local hotels and motels that were now owned by the government. After California became independent, tourism dropped by about sixty percent, and after the quake it dropped another forty percent. Most of the small hotels and motels went bankrupt and were taken over by the government. The same fate began to affect the larger hotels by September, so now there was someplace for the new citizens to live.

As the flood of new residents continued, a new problem appeared. Most of the families that crossed the border had school age children, many of whom didn't speak English. There was

106

suddenly a shortage of schools and bilingual teachers. Construction was started on twenty new schools, many of the buildings were formally factories that had gone out of business. That was the easy part, all that was needed was the money for construction. The harder part was finding the teachers. As the new schools opened, they were forced to use bilingual immigrants as teachers, even though many of them had only a high school education themselves.

Despite the problems, California presented a positive face to the rest of the world. By the end of August, diplomatic relations were established with most of the European countries; Australia, Russia, China, South Korea, Japan, Mexico, and Canada. The United States was the only major world power that refused to recognize California as an independent country. In September, 2025, they signed trade agreements with both Canada and Mexico, and began trade talks with the European Union.

The result of California's apparent success was that other states with left leaning governments began to feel they should also consider withdrawing from the United States. In October, Nelson Flanders, the newly elected Governor of New York, made a trip to California to discuss the possibility with President Peterson.

Adam found himself in a serious dilemma. He couldn't tell Flanders about the problems with the Chinese because he felt there was a significant risk the information could become public knowledge, but he had to at least try to convenience him that going it alone was a bad idea.

On October 8, 2025, President Peterson met with Governor Flanders in Adam's office. They had never met, but had spoken with each other several times. After exchanging greetings, Governor Flanders said, "I know you have had more than your share of serious problems, but everything seems to be going very well now."

Adam replied, "On the surface, everything does appear to going well, but please believe me when I tell you there are still some issues that need to be resolved."

Adam hesitated a moment, thinking that perhaps Governor Flanders would ask a question, but when he didn't, Adam continued, "Some of the more pressing problems are our inability to adequately house and educate all the immigrants that are asking to become citizens. Many of them don't speak English, so finding a job in the private sector is difficult. As a result, we have been providing jobs for able-bodied adults helping with the repairs from the quake. That is a significant drain on our treasury. We have converted many of our abandoned buildings into schools and apartments, but there aren't enough bilingual teachers. We have been cut off from the United States' electrical grid, and until San Onofre and Diablo Canyon are fully functional, we continue to have rolling blackouts. We are dependent on the Chinese for enforcement of our drug laws because we don't have enough police or the equipment required for enforcement. The biggest problem is, of course, the continuing repairs from the quake. Those repairs will not be completed for at least a year, and the cost is significant."

Governor Flanders, who had been smiling before Adam started to speak, now had a far more serious expression on his face. He said, "While those problems are significant, New York's only common border is with Canada, so I don't believe we would have the immigration problems you are experiencing. I believe we have sufficient electrical power generation capabilities that being removed from the United States' electrical grid wouldn't be a problem. And finally, New York is not likely to experience any Earthquakes."

"Governor Flanders, I can promise you that should New York declare its independence, you would be flooded with homeless people from the entire north eastern part of the United States. Also, you will be getting people crossing into New York from Canada. You won't have the language problem we have, and the numbers may not be as high, but you still have to plan for it. And, although you don't have Earthquakes, you do, from time to time, experience hurricanes and other violent storms that can cause significant damage." Adam paused, wondering if he should discuss China at all. Then he said, "But we were lucky. China provided us with the funds we needed for the quake repairs. In the event of a natural disaster, you may not find a wealthy benefactor like we did."

"Didn't the United States help you out when the quake happened?"

"Yes, but they pulled out immediately after we made our agreement with China. We now have most of the money we need, but what we don't have are enough people with the skills to do the repairs. I wouldn't count on the United States coming to your aid."

"I must admit, you have given me some things to think about. It's obvious this isn't something we should attempt without adequate planning."

"Absolutely. One other thing to consider is that you won't have a military. Even though an attack is unlikely, a military can serve other purposes. After the quake, I discovered that while Nelson was in charge, he disbanded the National Guard. I didn't find out about that until after the quake struck. I'm telling you this so you won't make the same mistake. In your planning, make sure you take into consideration 'worst case' scenarios. That way you'll be prepared when they happen."

"You were the driving force behind the drive to make California independent. So, I have to ask; are you sorry you did that?"

"Only time will tell if it was the right decision. Many of the revenue sources we were expecting did not generate the income we hoped for, and the quake would have drained our treasury if the Chinese did not help us. But despite that, I would still do it again."

"President Peterson, thank you for your time. May I call you if I have additional questions?"

"Of course. I'm having dinner tonight with Jean Foreman. She's a close friend and is in charge of the senate finance committee. Would you care to join us?"

"Yes, that would be very nice."

"Good, can you be back here at 6:00 o'clock?"

"Yes, I'll see you then."

Governor Flanders hired a limo for the day and it was waiting for him as he left the capitol building. He got into the back seat, glanced down at his watch, and told the driver to take him to Fisherman's Wharf.

As they made the trip from Sacramento to San Francisco, it soon became obvious that California was in trouble. There were people who appeared to be living under the freeway bridges, and there were open fields with tent communities everywhere. When they exited the freeway and began driving on the streets of San Francisco, the homeless problem was even more obvious. There were young children sleeping on the sidewalks in sleeping bags. There was garbage strewn everywhere. These people were living in conditions that were as bad as many third world countries. He knew the problem existed before California became independent, but it looked worse than when he had been in San Francisco a year earlier.

New York City had a homeless problem too, but the people were mostly out of sight. They were living in train and subway stations, where there was shelter and sanitary facilities. He wondered if New York would meet the same fate if they became independent.

He picked up his phone and called his assistant, Greg. When Greg answered he said, "After meeting with Peterson, and driving from Sacramento to San Francisco, it's really obvious California is not the utopia they claim it to be. Peterson warned me that we have to be prepared for the worst, and I believe him. I want you to meet with the committee tomorrow and tell them I think we need a minimum of two hundred fifty billion dollars in the treasury before we can consider withdrawing from the United States."

"Do you want me to give them specific examples of the problems, or will you do that when you get back?"

"Tell the committee we will need an Army to not only provide us with defense, but also help when a natural disaster strikes, and we will need a Navy to patrol our harbors and beaches to prevent drugs and other contraband from being smuggled into New York. That is in addition to the money I mentioned earlier."

"I'm sure you realize we don't have anywhere near that much cash in the treasury. How do you propose to get it?"

"At this point, I have no idea. That's why I want to make them aware of these requirements. Perhaps one of them will have a brilliant idea."

That evening at the restaurant, Adam, Jean, and Governor Flanders spent the first hour discussing many things, but there was no discussion concerning either California or New York until after dinner. Then Adam, looking at Governor Flanders, asked, "What did you do after our meeting this morning?"

"I had my driver take me to Fisherman's Wharf. The last time I was in San Francisco was over a year ago and I wanted to see if anything had changed."

Jean asked, "Did you see any changes?"

"Yes, the homeless problem appears to be much worse. The streets are filled with garbage, children are sleeping on busy sidewalks, the parks are filled with tent cities, and there are more panhandlers than tourists walking around the wharf."

Adam realized his assessment of the situation was accurate. He said, "Tourism has dropped dramatically since we became independent, and the quake made the situation worse. But we're going to be doing some things to bring the tourists back. In the legislature there are bills that will reduce or eliminate many of the taxes that were aimed at tourists, Disney and some of the other tourist attractions are going to lower their prices, and some of the airlines are going to have special fares between Los Angeles and major United States cities. All of the freeways are open again, and that will help too. But I know it's going to take time for things to get back to normal."

"I'm sure that will help, at least in Los Angeles. Are there any plans for San Francisco?"

"No, not really. We have to do something about the homeless problem first. Unfortunately, we have discovered that many of the people who are homeless are happy living that way. They like the idea of having no responsibilities and no need to work. They get free food, clothing, medical care, and for those who are addicts, free drugs. A policy I don't agree with, but the city is doing it on their own."

"So, San Francisco is a lost cause?"

"Yes, until the city wants to do something about it."

Then came the question Adam knew was coming. Governor Flanders asked, "Aren't you concerned about the presence of thousands of Chinese soldiers in California?"

Adam replied, hoping he could lie effectively, "No, not really. I don't think that presents a problem at all. In fact, it's probably a benefit. We don't have an army of our own, and I believe they would come to our defense if needed."

It was apparent from the look on Governor Flanders' face that he didn't believe a word Adam just said, but he commented, "I suppose that could be useful."

Then Adam said, "I hope you have given some thought to the things we discussed this morning. I wouldn't want you to make the same mistakes we did."

"Yes, I have. In fact, I told my assistant to inform the committee handling it that we must have a two hundred fifty-billion-dollar reserve before we can consider going independent."

"Will they listen to you?"

"There's no guarantee. The final decision isn't mine. We won't take any action regarding secession without the approval of a majority of our residents. If they approve it, we will do it. That's something California probably should have done. We have tentatively scheduled the vote for next April. That will give us enough time to complete our evaluation. And after my visit here, that evaluation will include some 'worst case' scenarios."

"Good, I don't want to sound like a boy scout, but it never hurts to be prepared." Then Adam asked, "When are you returning to New York?"

"Probably tomorrow morning. I want to thank you for your hospitality and advice."

"You're welcome. Please feel free to contact me at any time if I can be of assistance."

They left the restaurant and took Governor Flanders back to the capitol where his driver was waiting for him. After Governor Flanders was gone, Adam and Jean spent some time discussing the evening. In the end they concluded that they learned something from the governor's visit; they realized that living in Sacramento and working for the government isolated them from the problems that many California citizens faced on a daily basis. But neither of them knew how to resolve the problem.

When they arrived at Jean's house, Adam dismissed his driver. Then they went into her house where they spent the night together. Although they had known each other for years, their relationship had been strictly platonic, until now.

The following morning, Adam was surprised when he received a call from the director of the Diablo Canyon power station. He told Adam that they would begin testing the new reactor that afternoon and they were about thirty days ahead of schedule. He also said that if the tests went well, they could probably begin full operation in September.

It was the first good news Adam had received in a long time. He told the director to keep him informed and thanked him for the information.

That afternoon, at 1:00 o'clock, the new reactor at Diablo Canyon was started. Everything seemed to be going well. The reactor was functioning at twenty percent and the turbines connected to the reactor began to rotate slowly. The entire system appeared to be working, so the reactor power was increased to thirty percent. At that point the reactor cooling system power increased as well. Less than a minute later, the entire facility shook as a massive explosion destroyed the reactor cooling systems. All the reactors at Diablo Canyon were immediately shut down. The loss of power from Diablo Canyon caused the entire northern California power grid to shut down. Instantly, millions of homes and businesses were without power.

Nobody was injured in the explosion, but the Diablo Canyon cooling system was severely damaged. Fortunately, there was no release of radioactive material and the engineers were able to examine the damage almost immediately. It was obvious the damage was caused by an explosive charge placed in the cooling system output pipes. There was no doubt; it was sabotage.

Adam was notified a few minutes after the incident. He tried to control his anger, and knew there was no reason to be upset with the messenger, but he smashed the phone down and screamed a string of obscenities that would have embarrassed a coal miner. When he calmed down a few minutes later, he called Ellen and asked her to come to his office immediately.

"What's wrong?" Ellen asked as she rushed into his office.

"Some asshole blew up the cooling system at Diablo Canyon! We need to call a press conference for 4:00 PM and try to get President Haskell on the phone."

"Yes, sir."

Adam called his Chief of Technology, Bruce Carter. Bruce had worked for Adam since the early days of Peterson Gaming, and they had been friends for many years. When Bruce answered, Adam said, "Bruce, the cooling system at Diablo Canyon just blew up. I need to know as soon as possible how fast we can get it back online."

"Was there any radiation leaked? Do we know what caused the explosion?"

"I was informed the damage did not extend beyond the cooling system, so a radiation leak isn't likely. Apparently, the explosion was sabotage."

"Can I get a copter to take me up there?"

"I'll have one waiting for you at the airport in fifteen minutes."

"Good, I'll call you as soon as I have anything to report."

"Thanks, Bruce."

Adam called his secretary and told her to arrange for a helicopter to take Bruce to Diablo Canyon immediately.

Ten minutes later his secretary called to tell him that President Haskell was on the phone.

"President Haskell, thank you for taking my call."

"I thought we were on a first name basis, Adam."

"We are, Nancy. I'm so upset by the situation I can hardly control myself. There has been an explosion at Diablo Canyon. We were just starting to test the new reactor when the cooling system was deliberately destroyed by an explosion. Thank God there were no injuries, and there was no radiation leakage, but the plant is offline and almost all of northern California is without power. I don't know how long it will take to repair, but I'm sure it will measure in weeks, not hours. The reason I wanted to speak to you is that we need to get reconnected to the United States power grid, and I will gladly pay the United States any reasonable fee to make that happen. Is that possible?"

"Adam, I'm so sorry. It appears your problems never end. I'll contact the appropriate people and find out how quickly we can get California back on the grid. As for the charges, I have no idea what they would be, but I'm sure the same people are involved. Somebody will call you back shortly."

"Thank you, I really appreciate your help."

After President Haskell hung up the phone, she called Roy and asked him to come to her office. When he arrived, she asked, "Did we sabotage Diablo Canyon?"

"Well, not us personally. One of the California terrorist groups is responsible. We provided them with some information and nothing else. Why do you ask?"

"Because the cooling system there was just destroyed by an explosion."

"Oh! They must have started the new reactor."

"Yeah, they did. I am assuming you know more than you're telling me, but I really don't want to know the details. Please contact whoever you need to and find out how long it will take to reattach California to our power grid."

"Are they going to pay for it?"

"Yes, they are. They're also going to pay for all the power they use. I assume we have a way to do that?"

"Of course. I don't know what the charges will be, but I'll find out for you."

"Thanks, Roy. Please make sure President Peterson is kept informed, including the charges."

"I'll call him shortly."

That afternoon at 4:00 o'clock, Adam addressed the people of California from his office.

"At 1:00 PM the new reactor at Diablo Canyon was started. A few minutes later, when they increased the power output, the reactor cooling systems were intentionally destroyed as an act of terrorism. We were fortunate there were no injuries and there was no release of radiation. The area is perfectly safe. However, initial reports indicate it will take a minimum of thirty days to complete the repairs and bring the power station back online.

"In the interim, we have made arrangements with the United States to be reattached to their power grid. That will happen in the next hour. To prevent further problems that could be caused by power surges, power will be restored incrementally over the next ten to twelve hours, so everyone who has been affected by the outage will have their power restored by early tomorrow morning.

"Once again, President Haskell has helped us and we continue to owe her, and the people of the United States, a debt of gratitude.

"As I stated earlier, the explosion at Diablo Canyon was an act of terrorism, and I want the people of California to know we will take whatever action is required to determine who is responsible for this cowardly act and bring them to justice.

"Thank you for your attention. I will keep you informed as more information becomes available."

The next morning Adam received a call from Bruce Carter. He had completed his inspection of the damage at Diablo Canyon and wanted to give Adam his report. He told Adam the explosion was caused by a device that was placed about thirty feet inside the water intake pipe of the cooling system. It appeared to have a pressure sensitive trigger designed to detonate the explosive when the pressure increased to provide the cooling required for the new reactor. The explosive used was C4, which is fairly common and impossible to trace.

Adam listened to Bruce's report and told him to thoroughly check San Onofre and make absolutely sure there were no explosives there. Bruce said he would be there that afternoon and begin the inspection immediately.

XXII
Becker Aerospace
August 13, 2025

Harold was sitting in his office reading the LA Times when his phone beeped. He glanced down and realized he was about to get a call from Roy Stevens. He smiled, because he was sure this would be a new assignment for his people who had been getting bored waiting for something to do.

Roy entered the day's code into the scrambler and waited for the phone to ring. His wait was less than five minutes.

Harold answered by saying, "Good morning Roy, I hope you have something for us to do."

"I do. As I told you, your next target would be the Chinese. They are in the process of building five water wells in the 29 Palms area. They're also building a sewage treatment facility. We would like you to damage them enough to set them back a few months. It should be fairly easy because the area is not patrolled regularly, but there are no roads, so you will need vehicles that can traverse the sand in the desert."

"That's not a problem. Several of my guys have four-wheel drive trucks."

"Perfect. There's something else. The Chinese have developed a new type of plastic explosive, which we duplicated. It's several times more powerful than C4. I'll be shipping you some tomorrow. I want you to use it in your attack. I'm hoping they will detect the explosive used and blame their own people."

"That should really confuse them."

"Exactly. Make sure your demolition experts read all the documentation included with the new explosive. The detonation procedure is very different from C4."

"No problem. Do you have a date for the attack or is that at our discretion?"

"You should have your materials in two days. Try to get it done by the 22nd.

"That should give us plenty of time. I'll send some of my people out tonight to look over the targets."

"Okay, please let me know immediately if they find a problem."

"Of course, Roy. We won't let you down. By the way, I don't know who did the job at Diablo Canyon, but it was done perfectly."

Roy replied, "I have no idea what you're talking about. Goodbye, Harold."

Harold called his team leaders into his office immediately. When they were all seated, he said, "We have a new assignment. Our next targets are the water pump stations and the sewage treatment facility the Chinese are building in 29 Palms."

One of team leaders said, "Well, it's about time. I was beginning to think they forgot about us."

Harold continued, "I want three teams to drive out there tonight and check out the targets. I noticed someone posted aerial images of the area on the internet a few days ago. They should help you to find the targets. Also, we'll be using a special explosive that's being shipped to us. It's a Chinese design, similar to C4, but much more powerful."

"Can I assume they will be sending some technical information with the stuff?"

"Yes, I was told it requires a different detonation technique than C4. Okay, form your teams and remember our targets are in the middle of the desert. There are no roads, so use your four-wheel drive trucks. Report back to me tomorrow morning."

Everyone stood up together, replied, "Yes, sir," and left the room.

About a half hour later, Carl Hollings walked into Harold's office. Harold looked up from his computer screen and asked, "Carl, is there a problem?"

"No, I just wanted to let you know we located the targets on the aerial images, and we converted the locations into coordinates we can program into our GPS devices. I don't think there will be a problem, unless we run into a Chinese patrol."

"Okay, don't carry any weapons. If any of you get caught, just tell them you got lost or something. I don't want to make them suspicious."

"Okay, I'll pass it on."

Carl left his office, but Harold was beginning to get a little nervous about their current project. If his people get caught, there probably wouldn't be a trial. They would be killed. His people knew the risks involved with what they were doing, but that did nothing to relieve his concerns.

That night Harold went home to his empty house. He had a light dinner and went to bed early. His wife had been gone for more than three years and he missed her terribly. He was lonely, but the situation became worse when he had problems and there was no one to discuss them with. He was unable to clear his mind and relax. Hours later, he finally fell asleep. He woke up when his phone rang a few minutes after 6:00 AM.

Harold picked up his phone, saw that it was Carl who was calling, and was completely awake instantly. He asked nervously, "Carl, is something wrong?"

"No Harold, nothing is wrong. But the cell signal here is weak. I'll call you back in a few minutes."

Harold knew something was wrong. He walked over to the desk in his home office. The phone there was fitted with a scrambler. The phone rang about a minute later.

Harold answered with, "Okay, this is a secure line. What's wrong?"

Carl replied, "I was serious when I said nothing was wrong. Ted's team never got to their destination. His truck got stuck in the loose sand. A Chinese patrol came by and Ted told him they go out to the middle of the desert frequently because they were amateur astronomers and they wanted to go to an area where there was no light pollution. Ted had planned for the possibility of being stopped, so he put several telescopes in his truck. The Chinese believed his story and pulled him out of the sand. Then they left. They never even mentioned to Ted that he was trespassing."

Completely relieved now, Harold asked, "Did your team find the targets?"

"Yes, and they appear to be completely unguarded. Chuck's team found their target too. I don't see any problem completing the mission as soon as our stuff arrives."

"Good, thank you for calling. But you really scared me. I was sure one of the teams got caught."

"Sorry boss, I just wanted to keep you informed."

"It's okay, Carl. I'll see you at the office later."

At 9:00 AM Harold, Carl Hollings, Ted Porter, and Ben Johnson were seated at the table in Harold's office. Harold said, "Good morning. I know all of you were out very late last night, so I appreciate all of you coming in for the meeting this morning. I received a message indicating our explosive will arrive this afternoon. I would like to plan the attack for Saturday night. That gives us some time to get a close look at the new explosive we will be using. I want to emphasize that our job is not to destroy the targets, but make sure construction will be delayed by a few months. Ted, I know you didn't have the opportunity to check out your targets personally, and I don't want to send you out again. I'm going to ask my contact to get us satellite images of the target so we won't be completely unprepared. I suspect all the water wells are similar in design, so we can use the same plan for all five targets."

Ted said, "I'm sure you're right. I'm sorry I was unable to compete my mission last night. I thought my truck could go through anything, but I was obviously wrong. I'm having new tires put on the truck today that are designed specifically for sand. That should eliminate any possibility of failure during the mission."

Harold replied, "That's a good idea Ted. Let me know what the tires cost and I'll reimburse you."

"I needed new tires anyway, so don't worry about it."

"I'm not worried, I just don't want you to spend your own money for that kind of stuff. I'll be expecting to see the receipt on my desk tomorrow morning."

"Yes, sir."

"I think all of you should go home and get some sleep. We'll meet again tomorrow morning."

The three team leaders all nodded in agreement, then they got up and left Harold's office.

Once Harold was alone, he sent a coded message to Roy asking for the satellite images of the two targets they missed. The reply came back a few minutes later. Roy's message stated that the next satellite that would pass over the area would do so the next morning at 2:00 AM local time, so the images will be low contrast infrared. The next time a satellite passes over the area during the day would be at 4:00 PM the next day. He would send images from both satellites as soon as he received them.

The next morning when Harold arrived, he checked his e-mail. At first, he was pleased to find that Roy has sent the satellite images he promised. But as he read the message, he realized the news wasn't good. At the sewage treatment plant and two of the water pumping stations, the infrared images showed there were people there in the middle of the night. He couldn't tell if they were soldiers or construction workers, but it didn't really make any difference. They would have to be dealt with in order for the mission to be a success.

He sent Roy a text asking him to call as soon as possible. It was almost two hours later when he called. After Harold answered Roy said, "I'm sure you're calling about the images showing people near the targets, right?"

"Yeah, how are we going to deal with that?"

"I know your people don't want to hurt anyone if it can be avoided. I heard about something the Army was developing that I think will take care of the problem. It's a nerve agent that causes people who inhale it to fall asleep in a few seconds and remain that way for several hours. It's a very fine powder that's air dispersed. I know they were testing it a few months ago, but I haven't seen the results of the test. I'll find out before the end of the day if it works, and if I can send it to you."

"We would also need a way to deliver it. We can't walk up to them and throw it in their faces."

Roy chuckled and said, "Of course not. I think it was designed to be delivered by drone. Anyway, I'll contact you again in the morning and let you know what I find out. You will also get the daylight images tomorrow morning. Then we should be able to tell exactly why they are there. By the way, your crate will be arriving today."

"Good, I know Carl is looking forward to that. I'll talk to you again tomorrow."

At 9:00 AM Carl, Ted, and Ben walked into Harold's office. Harold looked up, smiled and said, "Good morning, gentlemen. I have some information for you."

After everyone was seated, Harold began, "The explosives Roy sent will be here sometime today. Carl, take a look at the specs as soon as it arrives and let me know if there are going to be any problems. Next, I received infrared images of the targets this morning. There's a problem. Three of the targets now have people stationed by them at night. I can't tell if they are soldiers or construction workers, but either way it's a problem."

Ted said, "I assume you don't want us to kill them, but we have to immobilize them somehow."

"You're right. We're not going to kill anyone. Roy believes he has a solution to the problem. I'll know more tomorrow morning. We'll also have daylight images of the targets then. That should let us know who's living there."

Carl said, "So I guess we'll be meeting again tomorrow morning."

"Correct. I'm expecting you to tell us all about the new explosives and I'll tell you what I found out about the people stationed at our targets and how we're going to deal with them."

Carl, Ted, and Ben left Harold's office. Harold turned back to his computer to read the latest news. Most of the stories were about how hard it's been for California since they became independent. A recent poll suggested that only a small majority of the people are happy with the current situation; forty-one percent thought secession was bad idea. Additionally, most felt that as time goes on things will get worse instead of better. The news pleased Harold, but there were still another nine or ten percent of the people to convince it was a bad idea to become independent. Then maybe an election could be held and California could vote in favor of rejoining the United States. But he knew that would never happen. Even if ninety percent of the people wanted to rejoin the United States and they voted to do it, he was fairly sure the United States would not agree.

He left his office a few minutes later, still thinking about what he could do to make the people realize that being independent was a terrible idea. By the time he got home he was sure he knew what to do and he planned on discussing it with Roy when he called in the morning.

XXIII
Sacramento, CA
August 16, 2025

Adam and Jean were sitting together at dinner. So far, they had avoided talking about California's problems. However, during a lull in their conversation Jean commented, "I know you use a limo instead of your own car now, but I don't have that luxury. On the way to my office this morning I stopped to fill up my car. Do you know the cost for a gallon of gas is now over twelve dollars?"

"Yes, I'm painfully aware of the situation. I don't see any way to get the price down until our refineries are fully operational again. That won't happen for at least another sixty days. It's probably not much consolation to know that gas in California is still a little less expensive than it is in Europe," Adam replied.

"You're right, I don't care what anyone else pays. I only care about the people in California. In July, despite the laws we passed about forfeiting ownership of your home if you leave the country without permission, more than three thousand families left. People can't afford to live here anymore. The middle class is being squeezed out. Ultimately, the only people here will be the very rich and the very poor. Our tax base is eroding faster than we can find new sources of revenue, and I'm sorry to say, our open border with Mexico is exacerbating the situation."

Adam frowned knowingly and said, "I know that. Thanks to the Chinese, we have enough cash to get us through for another year, or maybe two. But after that, without new revenue streams, we'll be in real trouble. We can't tax our own people anymore, so we have to find money from other sources. I'm open to ideas. Have you got any?"

"I wish I did. Both the United States and China have substantial cash reserves. Every time we try to screw the United States, they seem to be one step ahead. I suspect we could probably get additional cash from China, but the cost may be too high."

"I wonder how much they would pay for Catalina Island?"

"You're joking, aren't you?"

"Yeah, I suppose so. But the only thing we have to sell that has any value is land."

"Have you considered opening up some new areas for oil drilling? If we had our own sources of oil, we could significantly reduce the cost for the oil we buy for our refineries. If we keep the price the same, we could be making four, or maybe five dollars per gallon."

"Do you really think the people would allow us to do that? You realize the most aggressive environmentalists live here. If we tried to do anything like that, we would be immediately faced with lawsuits. Remember what happened when we tried to rebuild the Bixby Bridge?"

"Yes, of course I do. But we could eliminate the possibility by passing a law allowing us to open new areas for oil drilling without doing environmental impact studies."

"I hate to say this, but you sound like a conservative."

"I'm not being conservative. I'm being pragmatic. We have a problem and we have to find a solution."

"Okay, you use your legislative contacts and find out if they agree with your plan. I don't want to surprise the legislature with it."

"We have a finance committee meeting next Monday. I'll bring it up then."

"Okay. Do you have any other ideas?"

"As a matter of fact, I do. I think we need to find ways to end our dependence on the United States for our water and electrical needs. Hopefully, when Diablo Canyon and San Onofre are online, that will take care of our short-term electrical problems, but I think we need to look at other sources. Perhaps we could build a geothermal plant at Lassen. We could also find offshore areas where there are rough seas and build wave energy plants.

"But the water situation is far more serious. The United States could cut off the water supplies to southern California at any time. I think we have to get some of our best engineers working on desalinization systems that could produce enough fresh water to replace what we get from the Colorado River.

"I was also thinking about the possibility of setting up government run casinos. We could have both 'brick and mortar' and internet versions. Since we are no longer bound by laws of the United States, there's nothing preventing us from doing it. I believe that way we could bring in money from all over the world, not just from within our borders."

Adam though about her ideas for a few seconds before he replied, "I like the casino idea, but once again, you're going to piss off the environmentalists with your proposed power station projects. If you want to do them, the legislature will have to pass laws preventing legal challenges to any new public works projects."

"I think we can make that happen. Would you sign the bill if we pass it?"

"I can't answer that now. I would have to read the bill first. But I think it would be a hard sell. We left the United States because our people didn't like the way the federal government was doing things, and now we are talking about doing many of the same things. Just tonight you have talked about closing our border with Mexico and ignoring environmental issues for public works projects. Those are two things the people here care about deeply."

"I'm not so sure about that. I think the majority of our citizens care more about their financial problems than they do about immigration or the environment."

"It would seem that the only way to find out is to ask our people directly. I believe our citizens care more about social issues then they do about their personal finances."

"I'm sorry Adam, but I think you're completely out of touch with our people if you believe that, but I agree; let's ask them what they think is more important."

"Okay, I'll schedule a news conference for Monday night and ask them directly."

"Good, so now let me ask you about something that's important to us. Do you want to spend the night at my place?" she asked with a smile.

Adam looked at Jean and smiled back while nodding in agreement.

Russell Fine

XXIV
Becker Aerospace
August 18, 2025

Harold arrived at his office a few minutes before 8:00 o'clock. When he turned his computer on, he found a message from Roy that said he would call at 8:30 California time. Harold set up the scrambler and waited for the phone to ring. When it did, Harold picked it up and heard Roy say, "Good morning. Did your experts have an opportunity to examine the package I sent?"

"I don't know. I left the office early. Would you like me to find out?"

"No, that's okay. If they have a question or a problem just call me. I looked at the daytime images and it appears the overnight guests are all construction workers. I'll be sending you another present later today that will resolve the problem. Included is something to help with the delivery issue. Again, please look over all the material and contact me immediately if you have any questions."

"Okay, Roy. Now I have something I would like to discuss with you. I know you are being careful about what you say, even though this is a secure line, but what I want to discuss with you can't be coded in any way. Shall I continue?"

"Sure."

Harold continued, "Even with the big chunk of cash California received from the Chinese, we're still in trouble financially. I'm not sure you realize that gas is over $12.00 a gallon. Additionally, water and natural gas have increased more than fifty percent since we left the United States. The middle class, which pays most of the taxes and has very little extra cash, is being squeezed out of the country, and they are leaving in large numbers. I think that's a good thing, and I would like the United States to do something that would push even more of them out of California.

"As I'm sure you are aware, to prevent homeowners from leaving, they passed a law that required anyone who leaves California without permission to forfeit any real property they own here. That law has been somewhat effective, although more than three thousand families with homes left last month anyway. Part of the problem is that home prices have dropped about twenty-five percent in the last few months. That's something people who live here never expected.

"What I would like the United States to do is set up a program to compensate certain people for the property they lost if they move to the United States. I was thinking that it should apply to anyone who has any type technical expertise that's needed there.

"I believe that if enough people from the middle class leave, only the very poor and the very rich will still be here. That would force a tremendous tax burden on the wealthy, and they won't like it. It would also leave many companies here in dire need of mid-level managers. It may be enough to tip the balance in favor of rejoining the United States."

Roy replied, "It's probably going to be very expensive, but it may be worth it. I'll discuss it with the president later today."

"Thanks, Roy. I really appreciate it."

"I'll contact you again after I meet with the president."

Carl, Ted, and Ben showed up at Harold's office at 10:00 for their morning meeting. Carl had a big smile on his face. As he walked in, he said, "Harold, that stuff they sent is, by far, the most interesting explosive I have ever seen. It's detonated by applying an electrical charge to the detonators they supplied. But the interesting thing is, the voltage applied to the detonator controls the force of the explosion. For example, a three-volt charge attached to one kilo of the stuff would equal about eleven kilos of TNT. A ten-volt charge would create an explosion the equivalent of about forty-five kilos of TNT."

Harold grinned, "I'm sure you're anxious to try it. You should get your chance shortly. We now know the people who are at the target sites overnight are construction workers. They can't be harmed in any way during our attacks. The United States is sending us the material we will need today, and we should have it in a few days. Since you have never worked with this explosive before, I think you should do some testing before the mission. Do you agree?"

"Yes sir, I do. I must tell you the specs almost seem like science fiction. But if it works as indicated, it will completely change how explosives are used. It would be wonderful for road construction or mining applications."

"It makes me wonder why the Chinese haven't marketed it yet. Anyway, find some really remote location and do some testing in the next day or two. Let me know the results."

"That sounds like fun, sir."

"Let's meet again in three days. That way Carl will have the time he needs to test the explosive, and we should have the next package from Roy by then."

Russell Fine

XXV
Sacramento California
August 17, 2025

Adam had planned on a televised news conference to ask the citizens of California how they felt about Jean's ideas. But he changed his mind and decided to do it an informal meeting with a few of his TV and newspaper contacts instead.

In his office were two reporters from local television stations and the editor of the Sacramento Bee. Everyone was seated around the table in his office. They had already exchanged pleasantries when Adam said, "I asked you here today because I would like you to do something for California. Currently, our treasury is flush with cash as a result of our agreement with China, but that won't last for very long. We are depleting the treasury far faster than our revenue streams can replace it. As a result, we have to find new sources of revenue and ways to reduce our costs. We must also find ways to decrease our dependence on the United States.

"I have received several suggestions from the legislature. They include opening up new areas for oil exploration, building geothermal power stations, and setting up government sponsored casinos and internet gambling. These all have the potential to bring in additional revenue without raising taxes. Although there is limited support for doing this, many of the legislators also think we should be limiting the number of new immigrants we allow to cross our border with Mexico. They believe that would have a dramatic positive effect on our costs.

"I realize that many of our citizens will be opposed to most, or perhaps all, of these ideas. But I need to know the extent of the opposition. We're going to set up an online system that will allow everyone to vote on these proposals. They will need their voter registration numbers to access the system. The system will be available in a day or two, and we will send each of you the instructions on how to use it by the end of the day. You will also receive more details concerning the proposals. The system will be up for only ten days. What I want you to do is to let people know about the proposals and urge them to vote. Can you do that?"

Every one nodded in agreement. Then one of the reporters asked, "Do you mind if we add our opinion as to how we think people should vote?"

"No, I have no problem with that. I have my own ideas regarding each of these proposals, but I don't want to influence anyone. I want them to vote based on their own feelings."

The same reporter asked, "You do realize that if you try to do any of these things there will be legal challenges filed instantly."

Adam replied, "If we do decide to do any of these things, the legislature will pass laws to eliminate the possibility of that happening. I don't want a repeat of the Bixby Bridge fiasco. As long as we have the support of a majority of the people, I'm not concerned about any legal issues."

"So, if the people don't want any of these things, you won't try to push any of these proposals?"

"Yes, that is absolutely correct. But if all of these proposals are rejected, then we may be forced to raise taxes to keep California solvent. That's something I'm totally opposed to doing."

The editor of the newspaper spoke up, "I think we all understand your dilemma and I, for one, will do everything I can to help."

The two reporters agreed and all three left Adam's office. Adam wondered what the results of the vote would be, and more importantly, what he would do if all the proposals were rejected.

The following morning the news about the vote was everywhere. The newspapers, television, and many internet sites were filled with information concerning the vote. Much to Adam's dismay, most of the editorials regarding the vote suggested the people should vote against all the proposals.

It was the first time any country, with as many citizens as California had, asked the people directly about proposed legislation. The vote was scheduled to begin at 7:00 AM the following morning, and voter interest appeared to be high.

Adam looked outside his window and could see a slew of reporters waiting for him to leave the building. He had no desire to answer their questions. He knew they wanted his opinion on the proposed legislation, and he wasn't going to give it to them. As a result, he spent the entire day in the capitol building. By 9:00 PM the reporters had given up, so Adam went home.

The system was designed to give instant results as soon as the voters submitted their choices. By 10:00 AM, more than a million people had voted, and the vote was not going as Adam suspected it would. All of the proposals looked like they were headed for approval by a substantial margin.

As the news regarding the vote results spread, the extreme liberal groups, and the environmentalist groups, were already threating to file lawsuits to prevent any of the proposals from passing. They were accusing Adam of being a conservative, much as he accused Jean a few days earlier. In an interview that afternoon, he told a group of reporters that his personal opinion meant nothing in the current situation, the decision was in the hands of the California citizens.

That evening the TV news was filled with accusations that the United States had somehow managed to rig the vote because no real California citizen would vote in favor on any of the proposals. It made Adam somewhat angry that TV journalists would believe he would ever allow anything like that to happen. He was, and always had been, a liberal. But he was President of California, and he felt it was his duty to follow the wishes of the people, regardless of his personal feelings.

By the next morning, almost seventy-five percent of eligible voters has cast their ballots, and it was obvious that every proposal had passed. Jean was in Adam's office where they looked at the vote results together. Adam sighed deeply and said, "I guess you were right. The people care more about their pocketbooks than they do about the environment or open immigration. You have to start drafting the legislation that will allow us to proceed without legal challenges."

"It's already been started. The bills should be ready in a few days, and they should pass both houses without any problems."

"We need to get the legislation passed before the voting is over. I suspect, or at least I hope, that no suits will be filed until after the election is over."

"I'll see what I can do, but I don't think it will be a problem. I think this idea of allowing the people to vote was a very good idea. You are going to have to address the issue of possible United States involvement in the election."

"It's already taken care of. Josh Borden, the head of the IT group, has scheduled a news conference tomorrow morning to address the accusation."

"Unfortunately, many of these 'so called' pundits won't believe him, no matter how convincing the evidence is."

"Yeah, welcome to the real world," Adam replied.

XXVI
Becker Aerospace
August 19, 2025

Harold's team leaders arrived a few minutes early for their meeting. They sat down at the table and Harold said, "It's hard to believe, but the people appear to have voted for common sense. It's a refreshing change. I was thinking perhaps this will be our last mission, but then I realized that before the United States would ever consider letting us back in, we would have to do something about the Chinese. I don't think they would even consider having a Chinese military base on United States soil."

Carl said, "Perhaps our next mission will make them leave."

Ben replied, "I think it will have the opposite effect. They won't like being attacked, and it'll give them a desire for revenge. I think it will make them mad and they'll take it out on California. I have no idea how, but I'll bet they'll think of something."

Harold shrugged, "Regardless of the results of the attacks, we will carry them out. Personally, I agree with Ben. Anyway, we received some interesting items in yesterday's shipment. There were five drones that are capable of operating at range of up to 500 miles. They are almost silent. According to the information we received, they make about the same amount of noise as a small table fan. The drones will be used to deliver something they call *pixie dust*. It's a very fine powder which disperses quickly in the air. Anyone who inhales as little as one microgram will sleep for a minimum of four hours. The idea is to position a drone over the shelters the construction workers are sleeping in and drop the stuff. The powder is so fine it will be sucked inside the air conditioners and dispersed throughout their sleeping quarters. Ten minutes later we should be able get in, do our task, and get out long before they wake up. We can control the drones from here, so the teams won't have to worry about that. The one thing that hasn't been done is to plan the attacks. Our goal is to damage, but not destroy, the targets. Carl, how did your tests go?"

"I went out to an abandoned factory building near Riverside. The place was completely falling apart, so I figured nobody would notice any additional damage. I used one hundred grams of the explosive and detonated it with a 3-volt charge. The explosive was attached to an interior support wall that was made out of brick and was about one foot thick. When the charge was detonated, it completely destroyed a section of the wall that was about five inches in diameter. The stuff is soft and pliable, and is easy to shape into any form needed."

"Do you have any doubts about its ability to do the job?" Harold asked.

"No sir. This stuff is terrific."

"Good, now we have to plan exactly what we want to do at each of our targets."

Ben replied, "I looked at the satellite images of the targets. I think we should drop a charge into the well that will destroy the drill and collapse the hole. There's a crane and a backhoe at each site. We should damage those as well. In the case of the backhoe, we could destroy the drive tracks and damage the motor on the cranes. Those things can be fairly easily repaired or replaced, but not when they are in the middle of the desert. It will probably take a month to get them back in working order."

"That sounds like a good plan for the well sites. What about the sewage treatment facility?"

Ben replied, "Whatever they are doing at that facility is inside the building, and we can't see it. I think we'll have to see what's going on inside before we can make any decisions. Also, I'm not an expert on sewage treatment facilities, but the building seems to be much larger than necessary."

Harold said, "That's interesting, but I guess you're right. We'll have to wait until we get there to see inside and then we can decide what to do. I think one team should take the sewage treatment plant as a target, each of the other teams should target two pumping stations. Ted, since you are a pilot, I would like you to take care of setting up the drone operations. Start on that as soon as we're done here."

Ted happily replied, "Sure, that sounds like fun. It'll be like playing with a very expensive toy."

"I'm glad you're happy with your assignment. Since you will be leading one of the teams, you'll have to train someone else on how to operate the drones. I read a little of the technical manual last night. It looks like you enter the target coordinates and it will automatically go there, but then you will have to fly it manually to the actual target and drop the sleeping powder. You're going to need some time to practice. You have three days. Also, I don't want any surprises, so I'll ask for some new satellite images and we'll plan the attack as soon as Ted is ready."

Everyone agreed and the meeting broke up. Harold sent a coded message to Roy asking for the most current surveillance data on the targets. Now, all he could do was wait.

Russell Fine

XXVII
Sacramento, California
August 20, 2025

The news conference that Josh Borden held went exactly as Adam had predicted. The media people in attendance completely ignored everything he said. Their minds were obviously made up before they got there. They accused him of being complicit in rigging the election so the government would get the results they wanted, and the people would be fooled into believing that their opinions actually mattered.

Adam was impressed with the way Josh handled the meeting. He did it perfectly. He never lost his temper, or became obviously upset with the reporters even when they accused him of all sorts of things. When it became apparent they would not be able to fluster Josh, many of them simply left. When the news conference started, there were twenty-seven media people in attendance, by the end, there were only nine.

A few minutes after the meeting was over, Josh walked into Adam's office. Adam smiled at him, "You did a great job. You explained everything perfectly. The information you presented made it obvious that nobody could have interfered with the voting. The fact they chose not to believe you is not your fault. They are just a bunch of assholes who think they are always right."

"Thank you, sir. I appreciate your kind words and your candor concerning the reporters."

"You're welcome."

Josh left his office and was replaced immediately by Jean and Ellen. Adam waved them in and they sat down across from him at his desk. Jean said, "You'll be happy to know that the committees have finished the legislation and it will be voted on tomorrow. However, there are a substantial number of people who don't agree with the proposals, and they plan to vote against them. I'm sure the bills will still pass, but it may be close. I believe some of the legislators think like the media does. They refuse to consider the people of California would ever vote in favor of these ideas."

"As long as the bills pass, I'm not concerned with the margins. You know I don't agree with them either, but if this is what the people want, it's our job to make it happen."

Ellen spoke up, "I heard a rumor that some of the more aggressive liberals in the senate are thinking about having a recall election."

"You know what, if the people don't want me here, I'm happy to leave. I never wanted this job anyway," Adam retorted.

Jane held her hand up, "It won't happen, so I wouldn't be concerned in the least. By the way, did you watch Josh's news conference this morning? I couldn't believe those media morons were so disrespectful."

"I already told Josh he did a wonderful job. Anyway, I'm glad things are going fairly smoothly in the legislature. Jean, you asked me a few days ago if I would sign the bills if the legislature passed them, and I didn't answer you then. I'm answering now. I will sign them immediately."

"Thank you, I'll let everyone know. That will make it easier to convince some people to support the bills."

"You're welcome. I suspect some legal objections will be filed as early as tomorrow, so it's imperative we get this done as quickly as possible."

Adam was wrong about the timing for filing of lawsuits challenging the legality of the proposed legislation. That afternoon several were filed. Shortly after, Ellen came back to Adam's office to inform him about the suits. She also told him that she spoke to the Chief Justice who told her a law could not be challenged until it was passed. He also said he had already been briefed on the proposed legislation and he didn't believe that any of it was unconstitutional.

Adam smiled and thanked Ellen for the information, but he wasn't really pleased with what she told him. Although he felt compelled to do as the people requested, he would not have been unhappy if the proposals were deemed to be unconstitutional.

The following day all of the law suits were dismissed. The judge told the attorneys what they already knew: you can't challenge a law that has not been passed. He told them that after the law was passed, they were free to file their suits again.

That afternoon, several senators introduced a bill to have a recall election to remove Adam from office. The motion was defeated by a voice vote that was nearly unanimous, only the four senators who introduced the bill voted in favor of it.

Russell Fine

XXVIII
Becker Aerospace
August 22, 2025

Harold sat in his office looking at the latest satellite images of his proposed targets. The drill sites had not changed at all, but at the sewage treatment facility construction had started on five new buildings. It was too early to tell what they would be, but there were now guards patrolling the area. He wondered why a sewage treatment facility would need guarding. Perhaps Ben was right, it was more than it appeared.

Harold was waiting for a call from Roy and his phone rang exactly when it was supposed to. Harold answered, "Good morning Roy. I'm glad you called."

"I assume you have looked at the latest images of the sewage treatment facility."

"Yeah, I did. Why would they need guards there? Any idea?"

"No, not if it's really what they say it is. I also don't understand why they would need five additional buildings at a sewage plant."

"One of my guys said it looked too big for a sewage treatment plant. Additionally, sewage is traditionally treated by aeration, and they haven't built any facilities for that."

"We noticed that too, but we thought they could be planning on doing that later."

"Does this change your selection of targets?"

"No, but we have to know what's going on inside that building. I think we should forget about the idea of damaging it, and instead let's get inside and find out what they're really doing there."

"That sounds reasonable. I would like some night images of the area so we will know if the guards patrol at night too. If they do, it could make our mission much more difficult."

"I agree, it may be more difficult, but probably much more important as well. We're going to adjust the orbit of one of our satellites so it will be in a stable orbit over the target area. That way we can do constant surveillance. That should happen in the next twelve hours, so I may have additional data for you tomorrow morning."

"If the guards patrol the area all night, I need to know if it's possible to disperse the *pixie dust* high enough so it will blanket the whole area at the same time."

"Those drones have a fourteen-thousand-foot ceiling. So, height won't be a problem, but wind could be. If the wind is strong enough, it may blow the dust away from the area before it hits the ground. We'll have to adjust the height and position based on the weather conditions at the time."

"That makes sense. Won't the guards wonder why they fell asleep?"

"They might wonder, but they'll never say anything about it. If you were a guard in the Chinese Army, would you admit to falling asleep on the job?"

"No, I suppose not."

"Exactly, the guards will never say anything, not even to each other."

"With full time surveillance in place, we'll be able to watch the mission as it's happening."

"Absolutely, we can watch, but no communication. I don't want any radio transmission to give away our mission."

"So, no 'real time' images from our guys on site?"

"That's correct. We will have to be content watching the satellite images."

"Well, that's better than nothing. I'm anxious to see the night images as soon as they're available."

"You should have them waiting for you in the morning. I'll call again tomorrow."

After the conversation ended, Harold called Carl into his office. When Carl arrived, he said, "The parameters of our mission have changed. I want you to handle the sewage treatment facility. It's now being guarded."

Carl laughed and asked, "Are they afraid someone is going to steal their shit?"

Harold chuckled, "No, I suspect it's not really a sewage treatment plant. So, it's more important that we find out what they're doing than damaging the building. The mission is now to get inside the building and photograph everything."

"What about the guards?"

"We're working on that. They'll all be asleep before you get there. But you can't leave any evidence that your team was ever there."

"You know, I've done covert missions before. I'm sure we can handle this one."

"I'm sure you can too."

The next morning Harold was anxious to get to the office and he arrived a few minutes after 6:00. When he looked at his computer, he was happy to see that Roy had sent the images he promised. What he wasn't happy to see were the actual images. There were twelve images that were taken between 2:24 and 2:31 AM. The pictures showed four guards walking around the perimeter of the building. There were two other guards walking around the new construction area as well.

If there were only two guards to worry about, it wouldn't be a problem, but with six guards, the likelihood of them all falling asleep and ignoring it was slim, to say the least. It was still possible to stage the mission, but the Chinese would know someone was there. Because secrecy was impossible, he wondered if Roy would change his mind and scrub the mission.

Of course, it was obvious they weren't building a sewage treatment facility, but Harold wanted to know what they were building, and he was sure Roy felt the same way. He didn't have long to wait. Roy must have known when he looked at the images, because Roy sent him a coded message that said he would call in fifteen minutes.

When the phone rang Harold lifted the receiver, "Well Roy, it looks like we have a problem."

"Yeah, it certainly does. Now I am more curious than before to find out what's going on in that building. If they are that worried about security there, we need to move as quickly as possible. They may be planning to install some type of electronic detection equipment that would make the mission impossible."

"I don't think we can be ready for a day or two. We have to do some field testing on the drones, and I think that's going to happen tonight. If that goes well, we should be ready to go tomorrow night."

"Okay, I'll have a meteorologist here tomorrow night so we can give you the height and location for the drone. As long as the wind is fairly low and it doesn't rain, there won't be a problem. We should plan on doing all the missions then. Is that okay with you?"

"Absolutely, I'm sure the Chinese will increase security afterward, and then it might be impossible to execute them."

"You're probably right. What's the timing?"

"It's about a four-hour drive to the target area, so they'll leave here by 9:00 PM. What do you want them to do if they encounter a Chinese patrol?"

"Your people have military training, so they can make their own decisions. However, since we moved the satellite, we have had the whole area under constant surveillance, and there was only minimal activity except for the area around the primary target. Additionally, we can keep on the lookout for patrols and let your people know so they can avoid them."

"I thought you wanted to maintain radio silence."

"I do, but we can make innocuous phone calls. I'll send you the codes we will use to let your people know the location of any patrols in their area."

"I'm not sure there's cell phone service in that area. I'll check for coverage. If necessary, I'll pick up a few sat phones tomorrow."

"Perfect, I'll call again at about 7:00 AM tomorrow. Okay?"

"Sure, I'll talk to you then."

At 9:30 Harold called his team leaders into his office for a meeting. After everyone was seated Harold said, "The timetable for the missions has been set. We go tomorrow night. The drones *must* be tested tonight. The reason for the urgency is that it's now obvious the sewage treatment facility is something else. There are now six guards patrolling the area. The idea of getting in and out without leaving any indication we were there is no longer possible. There's some concern that if we postpone this, it will give the Chinese an opportunity to bring in surveillance equipment that would make our task impossible. The only thing that can delay us now is either a drone malfunction or the weather.

"The United States has moved a satellite over the target area so they are now monitoring it constantly. If they detect a patrol in your area during the mission, they will call you and advise how to avoid it. The message will be coded so it will sound normal, but you'll all receive the codes before you leave tomorrow night. I've already checked and found cell phone coverage is not very good in that area, so I've ordered a sat phone for each of you. They'll be here by noon.

"I want each you to go over your plans in detail. We won't have a second chance at this."

Carl asked, "Since it is now impossible to keep the missions secret, what do you think the Chinese reaction will be?"

"I'm sure they'll be angry, but I suspect they'll keep it to themselves. Whatever they are doing, I'm sure they won't want to discuss it. I probably don't have to tell you this, but you can't leave anything that would allow them to trace any of this back to us."

Carl replied, "We all understand. We'll be in and out of each target in less than 15 minutes. You said the United States moved a satellite to keep the area under surveillance. How do we know the Chinese didn't do the same thing?"

"We obviously can't be sure, but the United States has far more satellites than the Chinese. However, they won't be able to sneak up on you because we'll be watching in real time."

Carl looked at the other two team leaders and said, "Okay guys, let's get started," and the three men left Harold's office.

After they left, Harold really began to appreciate their bravery. This mission was not like the others. They were up against a trained army that wouldn't hesitate to use whatever force they thought was appropriate for the occasion. He only hired veterans, so they all had military training, but only a few had actually been in combat situations. Every one of his people was doing this job because they felt the government of California had betrayed them, and they wanted to do whatever it took to bring the current government to its knees.

His men spent the morning planning their missions and met with Harold that afternoon to go over everything. Harold approved their plans and as soon as the sun set, Ted and his team would begin testing the drones.

Harold read the manual that came with the drones and discovered they were very complex devices with amazing capabilities. Each one weighed about one hundred pounds. They were circles, about three feet in diameter, with five electric motors. Four of the motors provided lift and stability, and the fifth motor provided directional steering. The onboard computer was capable of moving the drone automatically to the programmed coordinates at speeds up to two hundred miles per hour. It was designed to be undetectable by radar, and it was almost silent. Once it arrived at its target, it could be slowly maneuvered to a more precise location. At its slowest speed it could move as little as ten inches per minute.

The drones were not passive devices. They were armed with two small missiles for either air or ground targets, and a transmitter that could emit a powerful electromagnetic pulse that could disable electronic systems in nearby aircraft or missiles.

At the end of the manual was a handwritten note from Roy, reminding the reader that the cost for each drone was over a half million dollars, and to please use them carefully.

After he finished reading the manual, Harold went home. He knew he needed a good night's sleep because he was sure that tomorrow night he probably wouldn't get any sleep at all. When he got home, he took a pill to help him sleep and it worked almost instantly. He slept until almost 7:00, which was very late for him. He showered and dressed quickly, and still managed to get to his office before 9:00. When he got there, Ted was waiting. He quipped, "Good morning, you're running a little late, aren't you?"

"Yeah, I slept late this morning."

"I didn't get much sleep last night, and neither did Amanda. We spent most of the night playing with the drones. Those things are amazing! We tested everything except the missiles. We did try sending out an EMP, and I can confirm the thing really works. I put an old notebook PC out in the middle of the yard. The drone was about a thousand feet above it. I activated the EMP pulse, and the

PC died instantly. It will never recover. The CPU is toast. I can guarantee there won't be any problems tonight. Amanda did most of the flying last night and she did everything perfectly."

"Well, Amanda was a fighter pilot, so that should have been easy for her."

"The drone is much easier to fly than a plane. It's basically like a big, flying, point and shoot camera."

"Did you try dropping a payload on a target?"

"Of course. You pinpoint the target with the onboard camera. It calculates the position the drone must be in to hit the target, it moves the drone, and drops its payload. We dropped a five-pound weight on a two square foot target from two thousand feet. The weight missed dead center on the target by less than three inches."

Harold smiled and said, "Wow! That's impressive. So, are you all ready for tonight?"

"All we have to do is load the *pixie dust* containers into the drones. The containers are altitude activated; they will open automatically two hundred feet above the ground. Each drone will have four of the containers, but I'm sure we won't need more than one at the targets, except for the sewage treatment plant, or whatever it is. By opening at two hundred feet, the dust should disperse over an area about one quarter mile square."

"To play it safe, plan on using two at the sewage treatment plant. One over the main building and one over the guard house."

"That sounds like a good idea."

"What time are you planning to leave?"

"We want to be within a mile of each target by 1:00 AM, so we're going to leave at about 9:00."

"That sounds perfect. Let's meet at 8:00 o'clock. We'll have real time access to the satellite sometime this afternoon. That way you can all examine your targets one more time before you go."

"Okay, I'll let the other guys know."

Harold's computer had access to the satellite by 1:00 o'clock, and he spent the next half hour examining each target. There was very little going on at the drill sites, but the sewage treatment plant was different. There were two large trucks stopped near the building, unloading large containers which were moved into the building. Then the containers were moved back to the trucks. Harold assumed the containers were empty, but there was no way to know for sure. It seemed like double work. Why not empty the containers inside the truck and just move the contents into the building? Then he had a thought; suppose the Chinese knew they were being watched by a satellite and didn't want anyone to know what they were moving. He also noticed that every box was unmarked. It just seemed very strange. In any case, he would know what was in the boxes soon.

A few hours later, he looked again at what was supposed to be the sewage treatment plant. The trucks were gone, and he was pleased to see only two guards currently patrolling the area. He hoped it would stay that way.

At 8:00 o'clock his team leaders arrived at Harold's office. He sent the output from his computer to the seventy-five-inch TV mounted on the wall so everyone in the group could see. Then they examined each target in detail. It was twilight, but everything was clearly visible. The work at the drilling sites had stopped for the night. At the sewage treatment plant, in addition to the two guards patrolling the area, there were a few other people moving around. They watched the area for about ten minutes and it appeared there could be as many as fifteen people there. Harold was silent, but he was concerned about the effectiveness of the *pixie dust*.

The three teams left the Becker Aerospace building at exactly nine o'clock. An hour later, Amanda began launching the five drones. By midnight, each one of the drones was within a mile of their intended targets. Now there was nothing to do until the teams were in place.

At 1:30 Carl called Harold and asked, "Hey, we're all at Kay's Bar, do you want to come and join us before last call?" That was the message he would receive if everything was going as expected.

Harold replied, "No, I think I'll pass. I found something interesting on TV."

"Okay, but you don't know what you're missing."

"I'll think about it, and if I change my mind, I'll call you."

Now, Harold set up his computer so he could view all five targets at the same time. There was no movement at all at the drilling sites, and at the last site there were now four guards patrolling the area. The guards had intersecting paths. They walked in a clockwise direction and each guard passed another guard about every three minutes. He watched until 1:30, then switched his computer to display the images on the conference room television and walked over to the conference room where Amanda had set up her five drone controllers.

Amanda was so busy when Harold walked in, she didn't notice him. He startled her when he asked, "Hi Amanda, how's it going?"

"Oh! Harold, you scared me. But, to answer your question, everything is fine. Just look at the monitors. The meteorologist just called and gave me the exact positioning for the drones. They are all exactly where they are supposed to be."

When Harold looked, he saw four images with a closeup view of the sleeping quarters at the drill sites. At the fifth he could see an image of the entire site. Amanda said, "The drones are all two thousand feet above ground level. The payloads have been primed and are ready to be dropped. That will happen at 1:55."

At exactly 1:55, all of Amanda's systems beeped and said, "Payload dropped."

Harold and Amada watched the display of the sewage treatment facility. There was nothing to see for about forty seconds, then the four guards all collapsed onto the ground. Harold said, "I guess that stuff really works." Then he picked up his phone and called Carl. When Carl answered he said, "The children just went to bed."

As they watched the monitors, they could see vehicles entering into the area of the first two drilling sites and the sewage treatment site. They watched as the three men got out of each vehicle and began preforming their tasks. They saw Carl and his two men walk into the sewage treatment building. A few seconds later Harold's cell phone rang. He looked at the screen and saw the call was from Washington. He answered and Roy said very excitedly, "We have a problem. Apparently, the Chinese are monitoring the sewage site with a satellite too. Our radar just picked up an attack helicopter leaving Edwards and headed for 29 Palms. It's traveling at about one hundred seventy-five miles per hour. It won't take very long to get there. We are in the process of notifying all your teams."

Harold yelled, "Shit! I was afraid this would happen." He was silent for a moment and then he asked, "Roy, do you have a problem with us using one of the drones to take out the chopper?"

Roy replied, "This is your operation, so you can take whatever action you feel is appropriate."

"When will we be able to see the chopper on our satellite view?"

"In about eight minutes."

"Can you tell which site the chopper is heading to?"

"It's on a direct course to the sewage facility."

"Thanks. I think we can take care of the problem."

As soon as Harold ended the call, Amanda asked, "From listening to your conversation I assume we have a chopper headed to the site Carl is at."

"Yeah, that's right. I want you to use a drone to take out the chopper before it gets to the site. Can you do that?"

"I don't see why not. I'll take the drone up to ten thousand feet, and I'll watch for the chopper. Do you want me to use an EMF pulse or a missile?"

"How close would you have to be to use the EMF pulse?"

"Less than three thousand feet, but that won't be a problem. They won't be able to detect the drone."

"I wish I had your confidence."

Harold watched as Amanda maneuvered the drone to ten thousand feet. Then she moved the drone ten miles west of the site. Until she could see the chopper on the drone's camera, she would not be able to activate the targeting system.

Amanda was watching the monitor, but saw nothing except the blackness of the desert at night. Then, even though Amanda did not see it, the drone detected the chopper and notified Amanda. She immediately switched on the EMF targeting system. The drone moved in the direction of the chopper automatically. Less than three minutes later, the drone had moved to within range of its target. It flashed a message asking for permission to fire the EMF pulse, which Amanda immediately gave. The drone fired the pulse.

As they watched, the choppers lights went out and it disappeared from view. The blackness had returned, but they had no idea what happened to the chopper. Then they looked at the infrared image. It took a few seconds to locate the image, but when they did, they found the chopper was still flying towards the target. Harold asked, "Can you fire a missile?"

"I think so. The missiles travel at about fifteen hundred miles per hour, so the chopper won't be able to outrun it." She switched the camera to infrared imaging, found the target, and fired a missile. Fifteen seconds later there was a bright flash that overloaded the infrared sensors on both the drone and the satellite. The chopper was destroyed, and Harold knew the Chinese would be livid.

Less than five minutes later Roy called again. He said, "The Chinese sent another helicopter to 29 Palms. You better get your guys out of there immediately."

"Okay, I'll cancel the missions to the other two drill sites."

Harold called all three of the teams with the emergency abort message, "There is a problem at home. Get there as soon as possible."

On the satellite image, Harold could see all three of his vehicles were headed out of 29 Palms. He kept watching until they were out of the area. He breathed a sigh of relief when he realized everyone had made it out safely.

A few minutes later Carl called. He said, "Hi boss, we're on our way home. I have some very interesting pictures to show you. Do you want to wait up for me, or should we do it in the morning?"

"I'll wait up for you. I'm anxious to see what you have."

All three of the teams returned by 5:15. They went to the conference room where Harold had coffee and doughnuts ready for them. They had all been up for more than a day, but nobody seemed to be tired. Instead, they were still excited about the mission.

Carl handed Harold the memory card from his camera and said, "You need to look at these. I have no idea what the machines in the pictures are, but there were radioactive warning signs plastered all over the place."

"I wouldn't think that would be needed at a sewage treatment plant," Harold quipped. He put the memory card into a computer and directed the output to the television. As Harold flipped through the pictures, he realized he had seen something like this before. The devices he was looking at were centrifuges. He exclaimed excitedly, "The Chinese bastards are setting up a uranium processing facility."

Carl stared at the screen. "What? Are you sure?"

"Yeah, I'm sure. I don't know what all of the devices are, but I can recognize the centrifuges."

"What do you think that means?" Ted asked.

"I think it means there are uranium deposits in 29 Palms, and that's why they were so anxious to get it. I suspect there's a shortage of it in China."

"Are they going to build bombs here?"

"Probably not. I would guess they want it for their power plants in China."

"Then why hide it?"

Harold thought about the question for a moment and said, "I'll bet their lease doesn't include mineral rights. I'll call Roy and let him know about this immediately. By the way, you all did a great job. I'm really proud of all of you."

Ted said, "Thanks, but we were are all happy that we can play a part in getting our old California back. I'm curious, you gave us all those code words so the people in DC could tell us where to go if there was a problem, but all our communication came from you. Why?"

"The communication protocols were set up to handle a Chinese ground patrol, not a helicopter. If the helicopter had spotted any of you, there would have been nothing we could tell you to do to evade them. So, the guys in DC told us about the helicopter, and we took care of the problem. Anyway, it all worked out, except for the crew of the copter."

"I'll bet the Chinese are really going to be pissed off," Carl said.

"Yeah, but they may not say anything, because they won't want to discuss their uranium processing facility that isn't supposed to be there. Anyway, all of you go home and get some well-deserved rest."

As soon as he was alone, Harold sent a message to Roy asking him to call, which he did about ten minutes later. Harold started the conversation by saying, "We know now why the Chinese were guarding the sewage treatment plant. It's a uranium processing facility."

Roy stammered, "Are... you... sure?"

"Yes, I'm sure. I'll send the pictures to you in a few minutes. Are there any uranium deposits in 29 Palms?"

"I don't know, but I'm going to find out. I'll get back to you shortly. I'll be waiting for the pictures. Don't forget to encode them before you send them to me."

"I'll take care of it immediately."

There were eighty-three pictures and it took almost ten minutes to run them through the encoding process. He sent the pictures to Roy as soon as the process was completed.

Roy called back about twenty minutes later. He said, "Back in 1942 they were searching all over the United States for uranium deposits for the Manhattan Project. Substantial deposits were found near the site of the Chinese sewage facility, but that information has never been released to the public. I would love to know how the Chinese found out about it."

"I'm sure they have spies, just like you do. Anyway, our question has been answered, but I don't think there's anything we can do about it."

"I'll let the president know. I'm sure she'll call Adam Peterson immediately."

XXIX
Sacramento, California
August 25, 2025

Roy was correct. A few minutes after he had briefed the president, she asked her assistant to place a call to Adam Peterson. It took a few minutes, but when Adam answered she said, "Adam, I realize that it's very early there, but some things happened in California last night I suspect you don't know about. I think you need to know what I'm about to tell you before you get to your office."

"I'm sure you wouldn't have called me without a good reason."

"You're right. I'm sure you're aware there are some insurgent groups in California that are very upset about leaving the United States. Last night, one of those groups decided to attack several construction sites in 29 Palms. Apparently, the Chinese were monitoring the area and they sent a helicopter to thwart the attacks. That helicopter crashed. I don't know if the insurgents brought it down, or it crashed due to a malfunction, but I'm sure the Chinese will blame you for it."

President Haskell paused for a moment and Adam asked, a note of anger in his voice, "How do you know about this?"

"We have satellites constantly scanning the Chinese facilities in California. Yes, our people saw the helicopter crash. But there was nothing in our scans that indicated the cause of the crash. However, the group that attacked the sites also took pictures inside the building the Chinese said is a sewage treatment facility and sent them to us. They were confused by the pictures, but our analysts were not. The building is a uranium processing facility. It was built near a substantial uranium deposit that was discovered during the early days of the Manhattan Project."

"Our lease agreement with the Chinese specifically said that with the exception of water, there were no mineral rights included with the lease."

"I'll send you the pictures, but I don't think it would be wise to let the Chinese know that you know the real purpose for the facility. I don't believe California is in any position to antagonize them."

"I'm sure I'll hear about the crash, but I'd bet they won't say a word about the sewage treatment plant."

"I'm sure you're right."

Adam asked, "Would you like to tell me what you know about this insurgent group that sent you the pictures?"

"It may surprise you to learn that I know nothing about them. Apparently, they went to the facility with the intention of blowing it up, but when they got inside and saw radiation warning signs all over the place, they changed their minds and took pictures instead."

"That was probably a good idea. Do you know what their other targets were?"

"I have no idea. They only communicated with us because they were concerned the Chinese may be building nuclear weapons."

"I'm sure they're not. I think they need the uranium for their power stations at home."

"That was our assessment as well."

"Thank you for calling. I really appreciate the information. I'm just not sure how to use it."

Adam was sure President Haskell knew more than she was telling him, but he was grateful for the information he received. He arrived at the capitol building at exactly 8:50 AM, as always. When he walked into his outer office, the Chinese Ambassador was seated and waiting for him. The ambassador stood up and said emphatically, "Mr. President, I must speak to you immediately. The matter is most urgent."

Adam replied, "Of course, Mr. Ambassador. Please come in. Would you like some tea or coffee?"

"No, thank you."

The ambassador followed Adam into the office and sat on a chair facing Adam's desk. As soon as Adam sat down the ambassador said, "Last night, two of our water drilling facilities in 29 Palms were attacked. We discovered the attack in progress and dispatched a helicopter with twelve men aboard to halt it. The terrorists shot down our helicopter and cost the lives of all those aboard. We will not tolerate this kind of action. There can be no further attacks against Chinese personnel or property. If this occurs again, we will take whatever action we feel is necessary to thwart the terrorists."

Adam was not sure how to respond. After a few seconds he said, "You have my deepest sympathies on the loss of your men. Our national police will be happy to work with your people in an effort to uncover the identity of the people who perpetrated the attacks."

"Thank you for the offer of assistance, but we will handle this in our own way."

"May I ask what you intend to do?"

"We will institute constant surveillance of the area, and anyone caught inside our territory will be prosecuted in accordance with our laws."

"So, what would happen to someone who accidentally crossed into your territory?"

The ambassador answered without hesitation, "Trespassing on a military installation is a crime is punishable by death."

"In the lease agreement you agreed to abide by the laws of California, which does not consider trespassing a capital crime."

"Our understanding of the agreement is that Chinese personnel must obey all California laws when they are on California property. However, on our property our laws are in effect. To prevent the loss of life, your people must be made aware of our laws."

Adam replied, "I thought 29 Palms was supposed to be a residential development, not a military base."

The Chinese Ambassador shrugged his shoulders. "We changed our minds." He abruptly stood up and said emphatically, "Mr. President, please do not be so foolish as to test our resolve in this matter. Thank you for your time and understanding."

After the ambassador left, Adam said to himself, *we're about to be screwed, and there's not a damn thing I can do about it.*

A few moments later, Ellen knocked lightly on Adam's open door. He looked up, smiled weakly, and said, "Good morning Ellen. I think we should all start learning Chinese."

161

"Would you like to explain that comment?"

"I'm sure you noticed the Chinese Ambassador just left. Last night there were attacks on two of their construction sites. They dispatched a helicopter from Edwards to halt the attacks and the helicopter was shot down, killing all twelve of the men on board. As a result, anyone caught trespassing on what they consider to be Chinese soil will be subject to Chinese laws, and the punishment for trespassing on a military facility is death. They now consider both Edwards and 29 Palms to be military facilities."

"So, if someone accidentally wanders onto their property, they can be shot?"

"It would appear so. But there's even more bad news. President Haskell called me early this morning to make me aware of what happened last night. There were actually attacks planned at three sites. When the insurgents arrived at what was supposed to be a sewage treatment facility, they discovered it was really something quite different. The place was set up to refine uranium. Apparently, the Chinese discovered that there are substantial uranium deposits in 29 Palms, and that was why they wanted it."

"You don't think they are going to build weapons there, do you?"

"No, but the lease they signed didn't give them any mineral rights, except for water. I don't think the facility presents any danger to the people who live in the area. The ambassador knows there was a third target, but failed to mention it. It simply proves they can't be trusted."

"From what you told me, I don't think the United States can be trusted either."

"I have no doubt President Haskell knows more about this then she told me, but I'm not worried about an attack from the United States. However, the Chinese Ambassador made it clear that if we make any attempt to stop them from doing whatever it is they want to do, we could suddenly find ourselves part of the Chinese empire."

"I'm almost afraid to tell you why I came here to talk to you."

"Is there more bad news?"

"Yes, I'm afraid so. The United States congress just passed what they call the California Immigration Act. The purpose is to make it attractive for technical and management people to leave California and move to the United States. They will be offering anyone who meets certain qualifications who moves to the United States a 'zero interest' loan to purchase a home."

Adam was visibly shaken. He said, "So, basically this circumvents the laws we passed to keep people here. Now they can simply abandon their homes, which are decreasing in value anyway, move to the United States, get a new home, and the United States government will pick up most of the cost."

"Exactly."

"Do you think we'll ever get any good news?" Adam asked sarcastically.

Ellen smiled weakly and replied, "We can always hope."

An hour later Jean called Adam on his cell phone. He answered, "Hi Jean. Today has been an awful day. I hope you have some good news."

"Sorry, I wish I did. Have you heard about the California Immigration Act?"

"Yes, Ellen came in to tell me about it right after the Chinese Ambassador threatened me."

"Why did he do that?"

"Because there were attacks at some construction sites in 29 Palms, and the helicopter they sent was shot down. Twelve of their men were killed in the crash. There's more, but I'll tell you about that the next time I see you."

"I'll come over this afternoon. Do you realize what this new United States program could do? Our tax structure is already hurting the middle class, and I suspect the reason many of them haven't left already is because of the real estate forfeiture laws we passed. Now, they have nothing to keep them here."

"I realize that. Let's try to come up with a plan to keep them here."

Jean replied, "I'll think of something."

Later that afternoon, Adam's secretary told him the Chinese Ambassador was waiting to speak with him on the phone. Adam was expecting more threats or other bad news, but he picked up his phone and said pleasantly, "Good afternoon Mr. Ambassador."

"Good afternoon President Peterson. I called to apologize for my actions the morning. I was overly harsh. I was very upset over the death of our soldiers. Our analysis of the explosive materials used at the sites indicate that the people who attacked our construction sites were Chinese, not American. So, for the moment, we will not be prosecuting anyone who accidentally trespasses on our property."

"Thank you for letting me know. I hope you find the people responsible. Have you found out anything about your helicopter?"

"We have removed the flight data recorder from it and are analyzing the data. It does appear it was hit with a high intensity electromagnetic pulse, but the helicopter was shielded against that kind of attack, so something else caused it to crash. When we find out what happened, I will let you know. Once again, please accept my apology."

"I understand completely, and your apology is accepted. Thank you for calling."

Adam was confused by the call. He was pleased that he would not have to issue a warning about trespassing on Chinese property. His dealings with the Chinese were minimal, but he had never heard about them apologizing for anything. Regardless, it was a pleasant change to get some good news.

Jean arrived a short time later. He told her everything that had happened that day. When he was finished, she asked, "Are we going to just let the Chinese take our uranium?"

"Do you want a war with China? I'm sure we would lose in a matter of hours."

"Don't you think we should do something about it?"

When Jean asked him that question, he realized why the Chinese Ambassador apologized. He wanted to end any discussion about the attacks. He was sure Adam knew about the uranium processing and he didn't want to discuss it. He was offering a trade, no trespassing deaths in exchange for no discussion about the Chinese stealing California's uranium. Adam was not sure who got the better part of the deal.

Adam replied, "No, we can't risk antagonizing them right now. As a matter of fact, we may never be able to risk it. We know the Chinese caused the quake, which in turn forced us into the lease arrangement. I think it was all part of the plan to get their hands on our uranium. But right now, they have close to ten thousand combat trained soldiers in our country. All we have are a few thousand police personnel and few, if any, have been trained for combat. We're training some people, but they're no match for the Chinese. They have played us since the beginning, and we have to play along."

"Do you think the United States would stand idly by while the Chinese take over California?"

"No, I don't think they would, but if there was any kind of war, we would lose either way. I'm sure there would be a lot of innocent people killed, and massive property damage."

Jean thought for a few moments and said, "You're probably right. Either way we lose. Our best option is to continue the way we are."

"Yes, but I wonder how long we'll be able to that."

Russell Fine

XXX
Becker Aerospace
August 25, 2025

It was early afternoon, but Harold had been up for more than thirty hours, and he was about to leave when he received a message that Roy would be calling in fifteen minutes.

The phone rang right on time. Harold answered with, "Hi Roy, I was about to go home."

"I know you've been up for a long time, but I just wanted to tell you a few things. Then you can go home and get some sleep. Is that okay?"

"Sure, a few more minutes won't make any difference."

"First, I want to thank your people for the excellent job they did last night. Our sources tell us the Chinese were so upset by the attacks they threatened President Peterson and the people of California. Then, after they analyzed the explosives that were used, they decided it was Chinese insurgents that were responsible for the damage, and the ambassador called President Peterson to apologize. During both conversations there was no mention of the uranium processing facility."

Roy paused so Harold asked, "How do you know the contents of their conversations?"

"I'm sorry, but that's classified information. I'm sure you understand."

"Yes, I understand. I was just curious."

"The next thing I wanted to talk to you about was your idea regarding enticing people to leave California. I discussed it with President Haskell, and she liked the idea. She asked some members of Congress to introduce legislation to implement it. I'm sure you'll be pleased to know that this morning the president approved the California Immigration Act. The basic idea was to circumvent the property forfeiture laws California passed. The way it works is; if someone has technical or managerial experience we need in the United States, they can apply to be accepted into the program. If they are approved and come to the United States, we'll assist them in finding a job in the area they want to live in. Then, if they agree

167

to come to the United States and purchase a home, we'll guarantee the loan, and any interest they pay on the loan can be deducted from their federal income tax. "

"So, the loan is at zero interest."

"Exactly."

"That's a good idea. You do realize the government here will do everything possible to prevent the people from finding out about this program?"

"Yeah, we are aware of that. President Haskell will have a news conference tomorrow and she'll be talking about this program among other things. Since it will be picked up by all the networks, I'm sure the information will reach the people of California."

"It'll probably force those morons in Sacramento to rescind those ridiculous laws."

"Perhaps, but our information indicates that most of the people in California are not happy with the way things are going there."

"I can tell you that from my own knowledge that is something of an understatement."

"I also wanted to let you know that if any of your people are interested in moving to the United States, their applications will be automatically approved. This applies to you as well."

"I may leave, but not until the government here is crushed. Until then, I'll do whatever I can to help you. I'll let my people know about the program, but I'm sure they all feel the way I do."

"Harold, go home and get some sleep. I think we'll be calling on you again soon, but the next time, all we will need will be the drones and the pilots. No other personnel will be required."

"Okay, Roy. Just call when you need us."

XXXI
Sacramento, California
August 28, 2025

Adam, Ellen, and Jean were in Adam's office for an emergency meeting. Adam started the meeting by saying, "Jean, thank you for coming on such short notice. I called this meeting because the response to the California Immigration Act has been far greater than we anticipated. More than six thousand people have applied to be accepted for the program in the last forty-eight hours. We have to do something, and we have to do it fast."

Jean nodded. "The easiest thing to do would be to repeal the real estate forfeiture law we passed. I could get that done in a day or two."

"I know that Jean, but I think we need to look at why that many people want to leave. Once we know that, we can take the steps needed to eliminate their reasons for wanting to leave."

Ellen stated, "I think the reasons are obvious. The taxes are too high. The schools are overcrowded, and the average class size is approaching forty students. To top that off, many of our teachers are unqualified, and most are being forced to teach in both English and Spanish. Since we changed the primary qualification for teachers to be fluent in both English and Spanish, the majority of the teachers we find are incapable of teaching anything more than basic reading, writing, and math.

"Our hospitals are overcrowded as well. The waiting time in most emergency rooms exceeds two hours. Every day, some of our people die while waiting to see a doctor. If you are unfortunate enough to need surgery, you're really in trouble. Unless you're going to die without it, you have to wait more than two months to have a surgical procedure. Hundreds of our citizens go to the United States for medical procedures every month because they can afford it, and they don't want to wait.

"Do you want more reasons? I can think of several more, but those are the most important."

Adam replied, "That won't be necessary. I think you made your point. Most of the problems you mentioned are the result of our open border policy. We probably screwed up right from the beginning. But even if we closed the border now, it would probably take more than a year to resolve the problems you mentioned."

Jean exclaimed, "We can't close the border! That was one of the primary reasons we became an independent county. I believe that the best way to resolve these problems is with additional revenue. We passed the laws we needed to create new revenue streams, now it's time to implement them."

"Okay Jean. What do you think would be the quickest to implement?"

"I believe we can have internet gambling up in less than two months."

Adam said emphatically, "Do it." Then he asked, "What about the geothermal power plants? Can we at least get a feasibility study started?"

Jean replied, "We've already passed the legislation to start the study. It should be on your desk tomorrow morning."

"I'll sign it immediately. Have you made any progress on new oil exploration leases?"

"No, almost everyone thought it was a good idea, and our citizens appeared to have no problem with it, but actually passing the law to allow us to do it is another story. I will have to sponsor the legislation myself, and I suspect the support will be minimal. I think passage is unlikely."

"Well, get started on it anyway. As you know, I'm not keen on that idea either. But, if the bill gets to my desk, I'll sign it, despite my personal feelings."

"Okay Adam, I'll get the ball rolling before the end of the week."

"Thanks, Jean. Ellen, I would like you to look into the amount of money that would be needed to rectify our education and medical services problems."

"That will probably take a month or two."

"I realize that, but we have to start sometime."

XXXII
The Oval Office
September 4, 2025

Roy arrived a few minutes early for his 10:00 o'clock meeting with President Haskell. He was excited because of the success of the California Immigration Act. He knocked on the Oval Office door and President Haskell called out, "Come in Roy."

The President was seated at her desk. She smiled at Roy as he walked in. He sat across from her and said, "The number of people who applied under the terms of the California Immigration Act has exceeded ten thousand. We're receiving almost a thousand applications every day. That number is far higher than we anticipated, and I'm not sure we can find jobs for all of them."

"I think that's good news. It means we can be very selective about who we accept. Has anyone done an analysis of the data from the applications?"

"I have someone working on it now, so I should have something later today. My plan is to start approving, or rejecting, applications early next week."

"Good, I would imagine that as their people start to leave, it won't take very long for the California government to notice. I'm sure I'll hear from Adam Peterson very soon."

Roy paused before speaking. "There's something else I want to discuss with you. I believe we must take action to put a severe strain on the relationship between California and China. I have an idea, but it could result in a Chinese threat to take over California. Are we prepared for that?"

"I've been thinking about that too. We would have to take action to prevent a Chinese takeover, but it can't be a military action. That would cause thousands of civilian casualties. So, the only actions we can take would be economic. We could threaten them with substantial tariffs, but that could hurt us economically as well."

"Have you thought about using the UN? We could provide proof they caused the quake that devastated Los Angeles. I'm sure they wouldn't like that made public."

Based on her experience as the UN ambassador, she had very little faith in it. It was obvious from the tone in her voice when she replied, "You're right. I don't think they would want the public to know about their uranium processing facility either. But the UN is powerless to do anything. They handle natural disasters effectively on occasion, but other than that, it's a total waste of time and money."

Roy leaned forward and revealed, "Actually, the uranium facility is part of my plan. I want to use drones to destroy it, and take out some other buildings at Edwards as well."

The president shifted her position. "I'm sure that would really piss them off and cause a substantial amount of friction between California and China. But I think the timing is bad. We have to postpone any action until after we've formulated a plan to deal with China."

"We can't wait too long. Once the uranium facility is operational, we can't blow it up without putting the people who live nearby in danger from radioactive materials."

"How much time do you think we have?"

"I've shown the pictures Harold sent me to some engineers, and the consensus was that it could be operational within sixty days. However, they felt additional electrical power would be needed before they could start the refining process. I'm sure they're correct because last week the Chinese asked California to supply additional power to the area until they can build their own power plant. However, the most interesting thing is, there has been no activity that would indicate any mining operation has started."

"Could the mine entrance be under the processing facility?"

"I suppose that's a possibility. The exact location of the uranium deposits was not pinpointed in the documents I read. If the mine is under the building, they could begin processing as soon as the additional electrical service is provided, and we would never know."

"I'll speak with some of my experts on China as soon as possible. Perhaps we can do something within the next ten days or so."

"Do you think one of us should contact Adam Peterson and ask him to delay the power line installation?"

President Haskell tapped her pen lightly on the desktop. "Roy, I don't think that's a good idea. The first thing he's going to ask is how we know about it, and I really don't think you want to answer that question."

"Yes, you're right. I should have thought about that. Give me a day to figure something out."

"Okay Roy, just keep me informed."

By the following afternoon Roy figured out a plan to handle the Chinese economically. He knew China's biggest trading partners, other than the United States, were Japan, South Korea, and Australia. He contacted the governments of those countries and discovered they were all very concerned about the Chinese encroachment into North America. As a result, they all agreed to halt all trading with China if they tried to take over California.

At their next meeting, Roy told President Haskell about the plan and she agreed it would be effective. As a result, she agreed to have Roy set up the attacks on the Chinese facilities.

That afternoon, Roy made arrangements to send Harold twenty-four missiles for the drones. These would be somewhat different. They would all be armed with the Chinese designed explosive that was used in the attacks on the drilling platforms in 29 Palms. Each drone would carry three kilos of the explosive and would be detonated on contact with a ten-volt charge. Making each missile the equivalent to one hundred thirty-five kilos of TNT. The targets would be completely obliterated.

Roy spoke to Harold the following morning. Roy said, "Harold, I think this will be your final operation. After these missions, we believe the Chinese will be forced to abandon their hopes of establishing a permanent presence in North America."

"What do you want us to do?"

"We want you to use the drones to demolish the uranium processing facility. We also want you to destroy several buildings in Edwards. We'll let you know what your targets at Edwards are shortly. I sent you missiles for the drones yesterday. They're all armed with the same explosive you used at the drilling sites."

"Won't the Chinese realize they're being attacked by California insurgents? That's going to really make them mad."

"Exactly, and we expect they'll use the attacks as an excuse to try to take over California. We won't let that happen. If they make any attempt to take over the government, they'll be isolated economically within a day. The United States and their other three largest trading partners have agreed to halt all trade with them unless they give up their plan to take over California. Once they realize their economy will collapse very quickly, they'll give up, and perhaps go home."

"It sounds dangerous. Sometimes arrogant people who are angry are incapable of thinking logically. They could react violently."

"We don't think that will happen, but just in case, there will be fifty thousand United States troops on alert and ready to take them on."

Harold sighed. "Let's hope it doesn't come to that. There could be hundreds, or perhaps thousands of civilian casualties."

"There have already been hundreds of casualties in the conflict with China, but you don't know about them."

Harold, almost screaming into the phone said, "That's not possible. How could that information be kept secret?"

"Only a few people are aware of this, so I must ask you not to divulge what I'm about to tell you to anyone else. Is that okay?"

Harold calmed down a little. "Yes, please go on."

"The Chinese set off a massive explosion in the ocean. That explosion caused a fault line to slip, which resulted in the quake that devastated Los Angeles."

Harold was silent for several seconds while he contemplated what he had just been told. When he regained his composure once more, he said, "The death toll from the quake is still rising. As they clear away the rubble, they are still finding bodies. The death toll must be close to a thousand by now. Do you think they did this just to get our uranium?"

"No, I think their primary motive was to establish military bases in North America. The uranium was a bonus."

"Don't you think the people of California have a right to have this information?"

"That's not my call. President Peterson is aware of it. It's entirely his decision to make. I'm sure he feels it's in California's best interest to keep that information confidential for the time being."

"Roy, I wish you didn't tell me. It'll be difficult, but I won't tell anyone. However, this information has completely altered my view regarding destruction of Chinese property. I still abhor violence, and I wouldn't take any action designed to purposely kill anybody, but if there are Chinese casualties as a result of our attacks, I would consider it acceptable."

"We believe it would be most effective if you hit all of the targets at the same time. To accomplish that, you will probably need several people trained on piloting the drones. How many of your people are already trained?"

"Only two, but we can train a few more over the next couple of days."

"Get started on that as soon as possible. The new missiles should be there by the time your people are ready. I should have all your target coordinates within 48 hours. I'll contact you again in a few days."

Russell Fine

XXXIII
Becker Aerospace
September 8, 2025

During the weekend, Amanda trained three more people. Harold's team now had five people who could pilot the drones. They were still waiting for their targets and the new missiles.

The shipment with the missiles arrived early in the morning. At 11:00 o'clock Harold received a message that said he would be called in a half hour. Harold's phone rang right on time.

Roy said, "Hello Harold. I received confirmation the missiles arrived this morning. I also found out something interesting. Our sources told us the Chinese will be conducting pilot training at Edwards starting this Friday. There will be at least twenty additional planes brought in for the training. The planes are a new design they want to keep secret, so the planes will be hangared immediately after landing. There are four large hangars at Edwards, and they will be your targets. I'll send you the coordinates for each building shortly. We would like to plan the attack for Saturday night."

"That won't be a problem. We have five people who have been trained to operate the drones. Is there an attack plan?"

"We're working on that. Our engineers are going over the structural plans for the hangars. They're looking for the most vulnerable spots. We think two missiles should bring down the hangars, so two drones should be able to handle the job. I would probably send an additional one as backup in case there's a failure."

"Agreed. Do you want us to hit the uranium facility at the same time?"

"Absolutely. That facility is much smaller, so one or two missiles should take care of it."

"Okay, unless we hear otherwise, we'll launch the attacks at midnight on Saturday night. Are you going to inform President Peterson about the plan?"

"That's not my decision to make. I'll discuss it with President Haskell. So far, she has requested not to be informed about attack plans, but this time it's different; this is an actual act of war, and I will not do it without her approval."

"Is the United States Congress aware of what we're doing? If this is an act of war, shouldn't they be informed as well?"

"Yeah, if it was a United States military action. But it's not. It's a covert operation by a California insurgent group. As far as I know, nobody in the Congress is aware of any of our actions. Actually, I think less than ten people know about our covert missions."

"I suppose the fewer people who know the better. I guess all we need now is the targeting information and we'll be ready to go."

"I'm sure I'll have that for you in a day or two."

Immediately after the call ended, Harold called his team leaders and informed them of the plans. He really wanted to tell them the Chinese were responsible for the quake, but he didn't.

XXXIV
The Oval Office
September 10, 2025

Roy had requested a meeting with President Haskell. He didn't tell her secretary what the subject of the meeting was. So, as soon as Roy arrived in the Oval Office, she asked, "What did you want to talk about?"

"I know you didn't want to be informed about our covert action plans, but this time I don't think I can give the order to proceed without your approval."

"I understand. What are you planning?"

"On Friday afternoon, a squadron of new Chinese fighter planes is scheduled to arrive at Edwards. Those planes will be put into hangars immediately to prevent us from looking at them with our satellites. My plan is to use Becker Aerospace to destroy the four large hangars at Edwards and the uranium processing facility on Saturday night."

"I assume they will be using drones for the attack."

"Yes, of course. I sent them missiles armed with the new Chinese designed explosive."

"How appropriate. I like that."

"I thought you might appreciate the irony. I'm sure you realize this is an act of war, and our allies are ready to take action immediately. We must be prepared as well."

"I've already alerted General Reynolds and he assured me our military personnel will be ready. You have my permission to proceed."

"Thank you. I also think you should inform President Peterson about the plan."

"You're probably right. I'll call him his afternoon."

"Thank you, Madam President."

Three hours later, President Haskell was speaking with President Peterson.

President Haskell spoke, "Adam, the reason I wanted to speak to you is that I felt you needed to be informed about the next action that will be taken against the Chinese. It will, in all likely-hood, result in a threat to take over the government of California."

"I must tell you that makes me very nervous. I assume you have a plan to counteract any threat they make."

"Yes, of course. If they threaten you, I must be informed immediately. Within an hour the Chinese will be informed that all trade with the United States, Japan, Korea, and Australia will cease immediately. I am positive that will prevent them from taking any military action. However, if they do, our military is prepared to immediately come to California's defense."

"Do you think the Chinese will leave California without a fight?"

"Our experts think so, but I'm not so sure. Any fighting we do will be economic. Nobody wants a shooting war."

"I agree."

"Adam, if they do threaten California, I think that would be a good time to mention the quake and the uranium facility. That might take some of the wind out of their sails."

"That's a good idea; I'll do that. Do you want to tell me the details of the attack?"

"On Saturday night, drones armed with powerful missiles will destroy four hangars in Edwards and the uranium facility at 29 Palms. We believe that at the time the hangars are destroyed, there will be a squadron of new fighter planes inside."

"That could cost them billions. I'm sure that will make them extremely angry."

"We're prepared, and now you are too. Call me immediately after the ambassador leaves."

"I will. I'm assuming you want them to threaten our sovereignty. What happens if they don't?"

"There will be more attacks on their facilities. The drones that are being used are undetectable by radar and they are silent. Basically, they are undetectable and therefore almost unstoppable."

"Who's operating the drones?"

"I'm sorry, I don't know. But, even if I did, I wouldn't tell you."

"I suppose it's one of the groups that caused us all those problems when we became independent."

"I really don't know."

"Okay, I won't press you for the information. At this point, it really doesn't make any difference anyway."

Russell Fine

XXXV
Becker Aerospace
September 11, 2025

Harold received a message from Roy shortly after he arrived in his office. The message read:

"No weak points found in hangar design. They suggest using one missile to blast open the hangar door and put the second missile inside the hangar. That should damage, or possibly destroy, all the planes inside. Each drone has four missiles, and because you have three drones for the attack at Edwards, unless there is a failure, you will have four spare missiles. I'm stuck in meetings all day, but I'll call you at 5:00."

Harold called both Ted and Amada into his office and gave them the details of the new attack plan.

Amanda asked, "What if the hangar doors are open? Can we fire two missiles inside the hangar?"

Harold replied, "I don't see why not. But these planes are secret, so I'm fairly sure the doors will be closed."

Ted said, "We have extensive satellite images of the area. We'll pinpoint the exact target coordinates today. We could do a dry run tonight just to make sure everything will go smoothly on Saturday."

Harold replied, "No, they told us the drones are virtually undetectable. It's the 'virtually' part that bothers me. If they somehow manage to detect the drones, the mission will fail. I don't want to take that chance. During the mission, if they detect one of the drones, we'll still have two others, so the mission wouldn't be a total failure. If they capture a drone, is there anything that could pinpoint where they came from?"

Amanda thought for a few seconds. "There are no markings on the drone anywhere. Additionally, we can activate an automatic self-destruct protocol if the drone has not returned by a specific time. The drones are pre-programmed to self-destruct if anyone tries to open them without knowing the proper procedure to remove the external panels, or if it is exposed to an electromagnetic pulse. There is no way the Chinese will be able to examine the inside of the drone."

Harold said, "Good, set all the drones to self-destruct if they have not returned here five hours after the missions start."

"Yes, sir. We'll do that."

"You said the drones would self-destruct if they were exposed to an electromagnetic pulse. What would happen if the Chinese sends out random pulses as a way to protect themselves?"

Ted replied, "I think that's unlikely, because that could damage the avionics in the planes at the base. However, I don't know the answer to your question. The drones are shielded, so a pulse would not cause any problems, but that's an interesting question."

"Let me know when you find out the answer."

"Okay."

Ted and Amanda left Harold's office. He could not help thinking about the possibility that the Chinese would react violently to the attacks. He was sure they could kill thousands before the United States could intervene, no matter how prepared they were. He was still thinking about that an hour later when Ted knocked on his door and walked into Harold's office. He said, "I got the answer to your question. The drones will only self-destruct if they are exposed to an electromagnetic pulse when they are not moving."

Harold thought for a second and then replied, "That's a perfect solution to the problem."

Ted smiled and said, "I thought so too."

Friday night Harold could not sleep, his mind was filled with the sight of dead bodies strewn everywhere. He had visions of Chinese soldiers running through Los Angeles carrying rifles tipped with bayonets randomly stabbing people who were walking calmly through the streets. He finally gave up trying to sleep at 4:00 AM. He left his house a half hour later, stopped at his local Denny's for breakfast, and arrived at his office a few minutes before 6:00.

He was quite surprised to see that both Ted's and Amada's cars were there. He went over to their work area and found them working on one of the drones. Harold said, "Good morning, you guys are here early. Is there a problem?"

Amanda replied, "No boss, but neither of us could sleep. I got here at 5:00 and found Ted was already here. We have to load the new missiles into the drones and we wanted to verify that they all had the latest firmware. So, since we were here, we got an early start."

"Okay, please keep me informed. If you find any problems, let me know immediately.

The day seemed to drag on, every hour seemed like three. By 4:00 o'clock all the drones were ready, six hours ahead of schedule. At 6:00 o'clock the other two drone pilots arrived. The five of them went out for a leisurely diner and were back in the office by 8:30.

The drone for the 29 Palms attack was scheduled to begin its mission at 10:30, the other three would take off at 11:00. All the drones left on schedule.

At 1:45, all the drones were within five hundred yards of their targets. Ted had two targets, and the other three pilots each had one. Harold, who was really just an observer, sat at the conference room table, while the four pilots were at their control stations. The wall mounted television displayed two satellite images; one showed Edwards, and the other showed the uranium facility at 29 Palms.

At 2:00 o'clock, the attacks began. All of the hangar doors were closed. Harold watched as the first missiles struck the doors; they were completely demolished. A few moments later the missiles struck inside the hangars. The initial explosions seemed small, but the fuel tanks on the planes exploded, starting a chain reaction. Within moments, all three hangars were fully engulfed in flames.

Ted maneuvered his drone to the second target and fired the first missile at the hangar door. When the door was down, he fired the second missile, but something went wrong. The missile exploded immediately upon release, instantly destroying the drone. Amanda saw what happened and moved her drone into position to fire another missile, but the drone was spotted by the soldiers on the ground who began firing at it. She just managed to fire a missile a few seconds before her drone was hit. The drone fell to the ground from a height of about a thousand feet. It exploded on impact. The missile Amanda fired did the job. Now, all four hangars were burning, and it was obvious anything inside would have been completely destroyed.

The uranium facility did not burn, but the building collapsed, and the delicate equipment inside was now useless junk.

The two remaining drones were now returning to Becker Aerospace. The mission appeared to be a total success.

At 2:30 Harold received a call from Roy. "Your people did a great job. I want you to know that no matter what happens tomorrow, we are fully prepared. Please don't worry about anything."

"Thanks Roy, but I am still going to worry for a while."

An hour later the two drones were safely back inside the building. The missiles were unloaded and stored. Everyone was exhausted, so they all left to go home and get some sleep.

XXXVI
Sacramento, California
September 13, 2025

Adam was expecting the call, so he wasn't at all surprised when his phone rang just before 6:00. When Adam answered the person who called said, "Sir, I'm sorry to disturb you so early on a Sunday morning, but I just received an urgent call from the Chinese Ambassador. He told me that unless you meet him at your office at 10:00 o'clock, a state of war will exist between China and California. "

"That's okay. Did the ambassador give you a number to contact him?"

"Yes, sir."

"Please call him and let him know I will be there."

"Yes, sir. May I ask what happened that could have caused that kind of reaction from the ambassador?"

"For the time being, that information is confidential."

"Yes, sir. I understand. I'll call the ambassador immediately."

"Thank you."

For most of the night, Adam had been rehearsing what he was going to say to the Ambassador. He was fairly certain how the conversation would go, and he was fully prepared.

Adam arrived at his office a few minutes before 10:00 expecting the ambassador to be there, but he wasn't. Also, since it was Sunday, his secretary wasn't there either. There was an intern sitting at her desk. As Adam walked in, she said, "Good morning Mr. President."

Adam smiled at her, "Good morning. When the Chinese Ambassador arrives, please bring him into my office."

"Yes, sir."

Less than five minutes later she opened the door and the ambassador walked in. He was obviously in a foul mood. He said angrily, "Are you aware of what happened last night?"

"I was informed there were some explosions at Edwards last night. Is that what this is all about?"

187

"Edwards was attacked last night by some highly advanced drones! They destroyed four hangars which contained airplanes valued at more than twenty billion dollars. I warned you before that we would not take any additional attacks lightly. We are now forced to put our soldiers on alert. Anyone trespassing on Chinese property will be shot without hesitation."

"I am sorry about the loss of your planes. I assume you feel California is responsible for your loss. However, your loss pales in comparison to losses we have experienced at the hands of the Chinese."

The ambassador, still angry, pronounced, "I have no idea what you are talking about. What do you think we did to cause that kind of loss?"

Adam answered calmly, "I have evidence the Earthquake which devastated Los Angeles was caused by the Chinese."

"We did no such thing! That's preposterous!"

"Not according to our scientists and geologists. The quake was preceded by a massive explosion on the fault line forty seconds before the quake occurred. That explosive was placed there by a Chinese cargo ship that stopped over that area for forty-eight hours, ten days before the quake."

Somewhat more calmly, the ambassador replied, "I don't believe that it's possible to create an earthquake. I am positive your information is false."

"I can assure you my information is correct."

"Even if you are correct, why would we do such a thing?"

"Because it was all part of a complex plot to allow your government to establish military bases on North America. You knew the quake would cause damage we didn't have sufficient funds to repair. Without your money, we would have been bankrupt. I thought your initial efforts to help us with our security and medical problems was a sincere effort to help us in a time of need. I now realize it was a part of your master plan. However, all of this has nothing to do with what happened last night. Whatever happened was not sanctioned by California."

The ambassador stared intently at Adam and said emphatically, "None the less, the people responsible are California residents, and your government is ultimately responsible for their actions. You should also be aware there was an attack in 29 Palms that destroyed a sewage treatment plant that was under construction."

"That seems like an unusual target for a terrorist organization. Perhaps they thought it was something else, like a uranium processing facility."

The ambassador was stunned and briefly unable to speak. When he finally did, he asked, "What are you talking about?"

"At the time you requested the lease on 29 Palms, I had no idea why China would want such a useless piece of property. We were monitoring the construction there and wondered why there was so much security at a sewage treatment plant. Then we found out. There are significant uranium deposits in 29 Palms, and you built your sewage treatment facility right on top of the them. I don't think that's a coincidence. Your lease does not grant you mineral rights, but I'm sure you thought we would never find out you were mining uranium. You aren't going to deny that, are you?"

The ambassador didn't reply. He simply stared at Adam. Finally, Adam broke the silence and said, "Mr. Ambassador, the Chinese have taken advantage of California, but that will not continue. We will, of course, honor our leases with China. However, we will not be providing you with any assistance. Within thirty days all utility service to Edwards and 29 Palms will be cut off. You will be on your own."

The ambassador smiled. "You are not in a position to threaten us. If we desire, we could take over California in a few hours. You have no military to prevent it."

"Should I consider that a threat, Mr. Ambassador?"

"Consider it a warning. Should there be another occurrence of destruction of Chinese property, our actions will be swift, and if necessary, harsh. Do I make myself clear?"

"Yes, but as I said before, the California government is not responsible for the actions taken by whoever is responsible for these attacks. You seem to feel we are powerless. I can assure you we are not. Although we do not have a military force, we do have allies that will come to our aid, should it be needed."

The Chinese Ambassador smiled at Adam again. "You are very naive if you believe that you, or your allies, would be able to prevent us from taking California. Thank you for meeting with me, Mr. President. I am sure we will be speaking again soon." Then he turned and left Adam's office.

Adam was wondering how well informed the ambassador was. Perhaps he was not aware of the cause of the quake, but Adam was positive he was aware of the uranium facility. In any case, he felt there was no reason to be concerned with an immediate threat.

President Haskell had provided him with a contact number, so he called her a few minutes later. It took several minutes to get her on the phone. After she answered Adam said, "Good afternoon, Nancy. The Chinese Ambassador just left my office. He was livid when he arrived, but after we discussed the cause of the quake and the uranium processing facility at 29 Palms, he became much calmer. That being said, he still threatened to take over California if any Chinese property is attacked again. He also said that anyone found trespassing on Chinese property would be shot."

"Do you believe he was aware of the quake and the uranium facility?"

"I was watching his face carefully as I spoke to him about what I knew. I don't believe he knew about the quake, but I was positive he knew about the uranium facility."

"Do you want to provoke them immediately, or do you think we should wait?"

"I don't believe another attack is necessary. I told the ambassador that in thirty days all utility services to Edwards and 29 Palms would be cut off. That was when he made his threat. I fully intend to go ahead with cutting the utility services, so it's possible that action could provoke them. I'm really concerned that if there's another attack they would react violently, and I don't want any of my people hurt or killed."

"I agree. I'll discuss this with my Chief of Staff. For the time being, I'll reduce the readiness level for the troops stationed near your border. However, please let me know forty-eight hours before you cut off their utility service. Adam, thank you for calling. I really appreciate it."

XXXVII
Becker Aerospace
September 15, 2025

When Harold arrived at his office, he was expecting a message from Roy, and his expectation proved to be accurate. Roy called about twenty minutes after Harold read the message.

"Good morning, Roy. Our mission was a success, but we lost two drones. One because of a malfunction that occurred when a missile was released. The other one was shot down. I don't know if the Chinese actually detected the drone or if it was just a lucky shot."

"I know. We were monitoring the signals from the drones. I called because I wanted to let you know that, for the time being, we aren't going to take any aggressive action against the Chinese. The California government is going to cut off the utility service to Edwards and 29 Palms in thirty days. We think that will be sufficient to provoke the Chinese into taking action, and we'll be ready to retaliate, economically and with force, if necessary. "

"Good, if that does provoke them, it may not be enough for them to consider military action."

"I'm not so sure about that. The Chinese Ambassador threatened President Peterson that any action, including cutting off utility service, would be sufficient reason for them to take over California. However, I would prefer to resolve the Chinese problem peacefully."

"Since we won't have any missions for the next few weeks, I'm going to give my people some time off. Is that okay?"

"Of course, your people deserve a break. They're doing a great job. Please don't forget about my offer regarding immediate acceptance into the immigration program."

"I've already spoken to them about it. If we're ultimately unsuccessful in getting the Chinese to leave, I suspect we'll take you up on your offer. But even if the Chinese do leave, California will still be in financial trouble."

"That's a problem we can't help you with. President Peterson and the others who pushed for California's independence are responsible for the problem, and they'll have to figure out how to deal with it. By the way, the immigration program has already enticed more than six thousand families to leave California, and we're processing requests for almost twelve thousand more."

"I'm sure it won't take very long for California to feel the economic impact from that. I'll bet most of them owned homes they abandoned, so the banks holding the mortgages and the local governments that are expecting income from property taxes are going to be in trouble."

"You're right. I don't know how much is left from the three hundred billion they got from the Chinese, but whatever is left won't last very long at the rate they're spending money."

"I wonder what would happen if the people here voted to rejoin the United States. Do you think we could become a state again?"

"I have no idea. That decision would come from Congress. But personally, I suspect if it did happen, California would have to agree to some serious changes in their policies."

"The idiots in Sacramento would never agree to anything that went against their ultra-liberal ideals. We had a vote a while ago regarding some changes to our policies of environmental impact from new public works projects and allowing additional oil exploration. The people voted for it overwhelmingly, but nothing happened."

"I guess the government always knows best, or at least the people in power believe that. I'll call you again in a few weeks."

XXXVIII
Sacramento, California
October 6, 2025

Adam, Ellen, and Jean were all in Adam's office for an update on the situation. Jean started the meeting by saying, "They found three more bodies in Los Angeles yesterday while rubble from an apartment building was being cleared away. That brings the total death toll from the quake to nine hundred thirty-one. Also, it took a lot longer than I expected, but the legislation that resulted from the public referendum finally passed. There are three bills for you to sign. As soon as you sign the online gaming law, we will get the contractor who has already been selected to create the software needed to get started. They estimate it will take about three to four months. There's also a bill to suspend, for a period of five years, the laws forbidding offshore oil exploration. The last bill eliminates the requirement for environmental impact studies for public works projects."

Adam breathed a sigh of relief. "I'll sign them all immediately. As you know we're scheduled to cut off utility services to 29 Palms and Edwards next week. I thought they would use the time to build some power generation facilities, but instead all they did was build an electronic surveillance fence around the entire perimeter of the base. By the way, the base has been renamed the 'Chinese North American Air Command'. They apparently have decided not to rebuild the so-called sewage treatment facility in 29 Palms."

Ellen looked at Adam. "I don't think they'll believe you will go through with your threat to cut off utility services. Perhaps we should send them a warning about the cutoff."

"I agree. Please send a message to the ambassador today. Use a courier, I don't want them to claim the cutoff happened without warning."

Ellen replied, "Yes, sir. I'll take care of it."

"Also, please arrange for me to make a speech tomorrow afternoon. I want to let the people know we didn't ignore the results of the referendum. Jean, I would like you to be there too."

193

"Of course. I'm fairly sure the people think we ignored their preferences. There's something else we need to discuss. Since the United States initiated the California Immigration Act, almost twenty thousand people have applied, and more than six thousand families have already left. We need to find a way to counteract the effects of that law. We have had several meetings to discuss it, but we haven't come up with a solution, or even an idea. Adam, perhaps a personal plea from you during the press conference tomorrow would help a little."

"I really can't blame them for wanting to leave. Real estate values are dropping, and taxes are increasing. However, I'll ask them to give us some more time to straighten things out before they abandon their homes. Anything else?"

Both Ellen and Jean said, "No," and the meeting broke up.

After the women left, Adam sat at his desk thinking about the Los Angeles quake. It was the deadliest quake that had ever occurred in California, and they were finding more bodies every week. The more he thought about it, the angrier he got at the Chinese. He wanted to retaliate somehow, but he was virtually powerless. His effort to bring them to their knees by cutting off their utilities was probably not going to be very effective, but at this time there was little else he could do.

A few hours later, he received a message from the Chinese Ambassador. It was blunt, and to the point. The message said, "Your action will cause a state of war to exist between China and California."

The message made Adam feel better. Perhaps his action would be effective after all. He asked his secretary to get President Haskell on the phone.

It took almost an hour, but when he finally had the opportunity to speak to her, he said, "Nancy, I received a message from the Chinese Ambassador saying that cutting off their utilities would cause a state of war to exist between California and China. I'm going to instruct our ambassador to the UN to request time to speak to the general assembly and tell them about the quake and the uranium processing facility."

"I don't think it will help very much, and it will cause a substantial amount of friction between your people and the Chinese. Your people will want to know when you found out and why you kept that information secret. Are you prepared to answer those questions?"

"Yes, I think so. I'll tell them that I kept the information secret to prevent any hostilities between California and China. We are ill prepared to go to war, and the people know it."

"Okay, that sounds reasonable. It's also true. But I would wait until the last possible moment to make any announcements. Ask your UN ambassador to request time to speak to the General Assembly on October 13th. That way, if China goes through with their threat, you will already be prepared."

"Thank you, that's good advice. I'll take care of it today. I'll call you immediately if there's any indication China is taking any aggressive action as a result of the utility service cutoff."

"We're constantly monitoring both Edwards and 29 Palms with our satellites. We'll know instantly if they do anything we feel is hostile."

"That's good to know. It's been a pleasure speaking with you."

As soon as he hung up the phone, he called his ambassador to the UN. When she answered he told her what was going on and that she should request time to speak to the General Assembly on the morning of October 13th. She was both horrified and angered by what Adam told her, and told him she would take care of scheduling the speech immediately.

Ellen set up the news conference Adam requested for 1:00 o'clock for the following day. Adam was seated at his desk and Jean was next to him, their camera crews were ready, and as soon as he received the signal, Adam started to speak.

"Good afternoon, I wanted to speak to you about the results of the referendum which was held several weeks ago. As you are aware, all of the items on the referendum passed by a substantial majority. This morning I signed legislation authorizing all of the items that you, the voters, approved. Seated next to me is Jean Foreman. She's the chairperson for the Senate Finance Committee and personally sponsored all of the bills I approved this morning. She has spent a lot of time pushing to get this legislation approved. Many of the people in our legislature believe they know better than the people they represent, and so it took longer than expected to get the approval needed to start these projects.

"The contract to develop the online gambling system has been given to GSI. They have developed similar online systems, so they are a logical choice to develop ours, and they are located in San Diego, which is another plus.

"UCLA has been given the funds to research the best locations for development of the proposed geothermal power plant. Additionally, all of the California based oil exploration companies will be sent maps showing areas which are now open for exploration. Please be aware that none of the areas we opened are visible from our beaches. Be assured that the view from them will not change.

"Updates on all of these projects can be found on the government website. As major developments occur, we'll send out notices to all California cell phone subscribers.

"Lastly, I'm sure most of you are aware there was an attack on the Chinese air base located at what used to be Edwards. There was also an attack on a facility at 29 Palms, which is now also controlled by the Chinese. Please be advised that the Chinese consider both of these facilities to be military installations, and anyone caught trespassing on either of those areas can be shot without warning. I urge all of you to stay away from those areas. There is nothing the government of California can do to protect you.

"Thank you for your time this afternoon. I will be speaking to you again soon."

XXXIX
Sacramento, California
October 13, 2025

At 9:00 o'clock, Adam gave the order to cut off all utility services to the Chinese properties. He had spoken to President Haskell's chief of staff earlier that morning. Roy assured him that the United States was fully prepared to engage the Chinese militarily if that became necessary. He also told him that Australia, South Korea, and Japan are ready to inform the Chinese that all trade will cease immediately if they make any attempt to take over the government of California. Adam told Roy that his crews were ready, and services would be cut off at 9:00 o'clock.

It didn't take long for the Chinese to react. At 9:20 Adam received another call from Roy. Roy said, "President Peterson, I'm calling to inform you that our satellite and radar systems indicated a squadron of eight armored personnel helicopters left Edwards three minutes ago. Each helicopter has the capacity to hold up to twenty soldiers, not including the pilot and copilot. At their current course and speed, they will arrive in Sacramento in about two hours. I'm sure they are heavily armed. Do not allow your security people to engage them."

"I promise you we won't make any attempt to defend ourselves. I don't want any casualties. I'll inform the security staff immediately."

"I also wanted you to know that our ambassadors have contacted the appropriate people in their respective countries regarding the cessation of trade with China. Also, our military forces in Nevada are on full alert. They can respond in a matter of minutes. Additionally, President Haskell has sent a written warning to the leader of the Chinese government."

"Thank you, Mr. Stevens. Please extend my gratitude to President Haskell as well."

"I'll do that. Please rest assured we are doing everything possible to bring a quick conclusion to the events that are about to unfold."

197

As soon as the conversation ended, Adam called his chief of security and told him what was happening and not to engage the Chinese under any circumstances. He didn't like it, but said he would do as ordered.

Then Adam called Ellen and told her what was happening and to make sure that everyone, with the exception of key personnel, should go home immediately. Fifteen minutes later there were only about thirty people left in the building. All the parking areas were closed, and signs were posted to inform anyone coming to the building that it was closed to the public for the day. Now, all they could do was wait.

Adam, Ellen, and Jean were waiting in Adam's office for the Chinese to arrive. They all guessed at what would happen. Adam glanced down at his watch and realized that his UN ambassador was about to start her speech. Although the speech would not be covered by live TV, there would be a video recording of it that would probably be broadcast all over the world in a few hours.

A few minutes later, they could hear the sound of helicopters approaching. As the minutes passed, the sound became uncomfortably loud, even inside the office. Adam had posted a guard at the desk in the lobby of the building. He gave the guard specific instructions to bring the leader of the group to his office immediately. As the helicopters shut down their engines, it became quiet again. All of them looked out the window and watched as the Chinese soldiers got out of the helicopters and surrounded the building. He saw two of the soldiers walking to the entrance. He was pleased to see that although all of the soldiers were heavily armed, they were not brandishing them in an aggressive manner. He was sure there would be no gunfire.

A few minutes later, the door to his office opened. The guard and the two soldiers walked into the office. The older of the two soldiers was obviously the commander of the group. His chest was virtually covered with medals, the other soldier had half as many.

The commander, looking at Adam, said, "President Peterson, I'm General Chang, the commanding officer of the Chinese North American Air Command. I'm sorry we have to meet under these circumstances. As you are aware, a state of war exists between our two countries. I don't believe either of us want this conflict. To prevent any escalation, I am asking you to resume suppling our military bases with the utilities which were cut off this morning."

Adam actually smiled when he said, "General Chang, it is a pleasure to meet you. However, I will not give that order. Additionally, even if I did, it would not be possible to restore services immediately. After the services were cut, the valves that supply the water to your bases were welded shut. They cannot be turned on; they have to be replaced. My engineers tell me it would take more than a week. The electrical service to your air base is supplied through an electrical substation about a half mile from the base. That substation was destroyed in an explosion this morning."

"I assume that the substation was intentionally destroyed."

"That is correct, General".

"President Peterson, you leave me no choice. I am placing you under arrest."

"What are the charges?"

"No charges are required. You are the leader of our enemy in a of time war, and as such, you are subject to arrest."

"I understand General, but I don't believe you are fully aware of the extenuating circumstances. I understand you feel that we, in some way, violated our agreement with you. However, at this moment, California's ambassador to the United Nations is explaining to the General Assembly that China deliberately caused the Earthquake that destroyed a large portion of Los Angeles. She has proof which she will show them. Also, she will show that China violated the lease agreement for 29 Palms. That lease specifically stated that no mineral rights, with the exception of water, were granted in the lease, and China attempted to start a uranium mining operation under a building that we were told was a sewage treatment facility.

"Additionally, we have an agreement with the United States, Australia, South Korea, and Japan which states that all trade with China will be terminated immediately if China makes any attempt to replace the government in California.

"Finally, the United States has a substantial military force just over our border in Nevada. They are on alert status, and will prevent any hostilities from occurring. So, knowing this, if you still want to place me under arrest, I will not resist."

General Chang was obviously caught off guard. The look on his face made it was obvious he was fully aware of both the Earthquake and the Uranium mining operation. He said nothing for several seconds. Then he said, "I will have to discuss this with my superiors. Please excuse me." He turned around and left Adam's office, the other soldier followed closely behind.

Ellen looked at Adam and Jean. "What do you think will happen now?"

"I have no idea. China's economy is almost completely dependent on foreign trade. The General knows that, so I suspect he's going to attempt to validate what I just told him."

Jean asked, "Is everything you told him true?"

"Yes, both President Haskell and Roy Stevens assured me that everything I told the General was correct."

Ellen said, "Assuming you aren't arrested, you're going to have to tell the people of California everything that happened, probably before our UN speech is made public."

"You're right. I have to do that. Jean, in the event I'm arrested, the responsibility will be yours."

At that moment the engines of the helicopters started again. Ten minutes later they were gone. As they watched the helicopters leave, Adam sighed deeply and said, "I guess I'll never get to see the inside of a Chinese jail cell."

Ellen smiled and asked, "That's a good thing, isn't it?"

"Yes. I didn't think it would come to that anyway, but I'm glad it's over."

Jean shook her head and said, "It's not over. The Chinese are still here. This may be only the first skirmish. The real battle may still come."

"Jean, you have no idea how much I want you to be wrong. I'll admit today's events were not the problem I imagined they would be, but I don't think the Chinese are going to leave California very soon. They've invested millions of dollars already making improvements at Edwards, and they have several construction projects going on at 29 Palms, not counting the now demolished uranium processing facility. It'll take some pressure from other countries to make them leave. I think our best hope is condemnation from the members of the UN General Assembly who will cease trade with them because of the Los Angeles quake."

Ellen asked, "Do you think that will happen?"

"At the end of the speech at the UN today, our ambassador asked the other UN members to do exactly that. But, of course, that doesn't mean they'll do it. I suspect that before they take any action, they'll first examine all the consequences of ceasing trade with China, and they will only do it if it makes sense financially."

"I'm sure we would do the same if China had attacked another country and they asked for our help," Jean replied.

Adam simply nodded his head in agreement. "Ellen, I have to make a public announcement tonight. Please set it up for this evening."

"Okay, I'll take care of it. Will you be ready by 6:00 o'clock?"

"Yes, I'll be ready."

At 6:00 o'clock, all the local television stations interrupted their news broadcasts to give Adam a few minutes to talk to the people of California. He gave them a brief synopsis of what happened, explained when he found out the Chinese caused the Los Angeles quake, and why he felt it was necessary to keep it secret at that time.

The reaction from the California citizens was mostly positive, and Adam was pleased the people understood and approved of his decisions in the matter.

XXXX
The Oval Office
October 14, 2025

Roy and President Haskell had a 1:00 PM meeting scheduled, and Roy arrived a few minutes late. When he knocked on the door, President Haskell glanced up at the big grandfather clock and noted that Roy was late, which was very unusual. She called out, "Come in, Roy."

Roy walked into her office and said, "I'm sorry I'm late. I've been on the phone all morning trying to line up support to strangle China's trade with the rest of the world."

"How's it going?"

"Actually, better than I expected. Canada, the UK, and France all agreed to eliminate, or at least reduce, trade with China. Germany wants a few days to study the issue before they make any commitment. China is Mexico's largest trading partner. They get most of their oil from Mexico, and Mexico isn't going to do anything to alter that."

"Do you think we've lined up enough support to make the Chinese leave California?"

"No, not yet. However, almost all the members of the United Nations were horrified to discover the Chinese intentionally created the quake that nearly destroyed Los Angeles. I think over the next few days there will be additional support for the economic isolation of China. I'm surprised China never even made an effort to deny the allegations."

"I've instructed all of our ambassadors to the smaller countries to pressure their contacts to push for elimination of Chinese trade. I hope we'll get some results from that in the next few days."

Then Roy asked a question that had been bothering him for days. "What are you going to do if California askes to be readmitted to the United States?"

"I've been thinking about that for the last several days. I suspect it's going to happen shortly after China leaves. We would never allow any foreign power, even a friendly one, to have a military base on American soil. I'm sure President Peterson realizes that. Do you have any suggestions?"

"Their withdrawal from the United States has cost us billions of dollars. I don't think they should be readmitted unless they agree to pay us back."

"You know they can't afford it. The only reason they would ask to be readmitted would be to avert a financial disaster."

"Perhaps you should discuss it with President Peterson the next time you speak with him," Roy suggested.

"I think I'd prefer to wait until he asks. In the meantime, why don't you speak with some of our people in congress and find out what they think about the subject?"

"Okay, I'll do that over the next few days. I'll let you know what I find out."

"Thanks, Roy."

XXXXI
Sacramento, California
October 20, 2025

It had been a week since the attempted coup by the Chinese. Adam had expected to hear something from them before the end of the previous week, but there had been no communication with the Chinese since General Chang left his office. So, Adam was not surprised to see the Chinese ambassador waiting for him when he arrived at his office.

"Good morning, Mr. Ambassador. Is there something on your mind you would like to discuss?"

"Yes, Mr. President. May I come into your office so we may speak privately?"

"Of course," Adam said. He walked over to his office door and held it open for the Ambassador. Adam sat down at his desk, and the Ambassador sat on the chair in front of it. "What would you like to talk about?" Adam asked.

The ambassador smiled weakly and said, "I am here to apologize for our actions. I was completely unaware China was responsible for the Earthquake that devastated Los Angeles. That action was not approved by the Chinese government. It was the action of a renegade general who has since been relieved of his command and is facing charges that will probably result is his execution. This man was General Chang's superior, and General Chang will be replacing him immediately.

"I was not initially aware of the uranium processing facility at 29 Palms. I was informed about it two weeks ago. As you probably know, that facility has been abandoned. It will not be rebuilt.

"China is facing serious economic problems as a direct result of our actions. In order to resolve these problems, we will be vacating our facility at Edwards within two weeks. We would like to continue the development at 29 Palms. It was going to be a residential development, and with your permission, we will continue the construction there. As I'm sure you know, many of our larger cities are overcrowded, and the air is polluted. We would like to provide a place where some of our city dwellers can go to get away from the crowds and breathe fresh air."

Adam replied, "Mr. Ambassador, thank you for your candor. Can I assume there will be no military personnel stationed at 29 Palms?"

"Yes, there will be a small police force, but no soldiers. Also, it will be open so anyone will be able to visit the area. We will have to build a sewage treatment facility, but this time it will be a real one."

"Are you expecting us to return any of the money you gave us for the leases?"

"No, the money is yours. Additionally, with your approval, we would like to assist you in rebuilding the areas devastated by the quake."

"Thank you, we appreciate all the help we can get."

"So, Mr. President, will you approve our request to continue construction at 29 Palms?"

"I would like to see the plans first, but I don't think it will be a problem."

"Thank you, Mr. President. I will have the plans sent over as soon as possible. We will wait for your approval before we start any construction projects. Also, please let me know who to contact so we can assist in Los Angeles."

Adam wrote something on a notepad, tore off the top sheet, and handed it to the ambassador. He said, "Jim Fontaine is in charge of the Los Angeles rebuilding effort. He can tell you where your people would be most helpful."

The ambassador took the note and glanced down at it. "Thank you for your time, Mr. President. We will contact Mr. Fontaine this afternoon."

"Thank you, Mr. Ambassador."

As soon as the ambassador left, Adam called Ellen and asked her to come to his office. As she walked in Adam said, "You won't believe what just happened." Then he proceeded to tell her about the ambassador's visit.

Ellen listen to everything Adam said and it all sounded so positive, but something was still bothering her. She asked, "How do you know you can trust them? They've lied to us constantly."

"I'm not positive we can trust them yet. However, I have little choice in the matter. Don't forget, they have a substantial military force and we have none. If we do something to really piss them off, California could become New China in a matter of hours. Also, they could demand that we repay the three hundred billion dollars we received, and we don't have the money anymore. Finally, look on the bright side. If they are telling us the truth and they build a real residential development at 29 Palms, it will be a big boost to our economy. Even if they don't pay taxes, they'll be buying things from California companies for the construction, and possibly use California construction workers as well."

Ellen said, "Okay, I'll try to be optimistic about the situation. I think the next time you speak to the Chinese ambassador you should make it clear you are expecting them to use California companies to supply the building materials they will need, and use California construction workers as well."

"You're right. I'll speak to the ambassador about it the next time I see him."

"So, I guess we won this battle. I'm hoping it will be the last one."

"Yes," Adam agreed, "But we still have a boatload of problems, and most of them are financial."

"The online gaming system should begin producing income in about two months, and we still have plenty of the cash we received from the Chinese."

"I know that, and the other two projects will help out as well. But I suspect we won't see a dime from either one of them for two years. Also, I now realize that we must have a military force of our own. We can't depend on the United States to defend us in the future. I have no idea what the cost of that would be."

Ellen was silent for a few moments, then she said thoughtfully, "Perhaps we should consider rejoining the United States."

Adam chuckled slightly and replied, "I wish it was that easy. Don't think that I haven't considered that possibility. But I don't believe they're anxious to take us back. With the Chinese leaving Edwards, there is some possibility it could happen. But this time we have to have a public referendum. I want the people to decide this time, not the politicians."

"Perhaps we could leak it to the press that we are considering it. That would give us an opportunity to find out what people think about the idea."

"That's a good idea. I'm sure you have some media contacts who could do that for us. Also, I have to let the people know what the Chinese are doing, so please set up another public announcement like you did last week."

"I'll take care of it."

This time Adam recorded the announcement early in the afternoon and sent copies of it to all the local television stations. In addition to informing the public about the Chinese, he also told them it was possible California would be facing a financial problem soon unless spending was cut or additional sources of revenue were found. He also said the online gaming system would begin to produce revenue in less than two months and that would help, but it would not be enough to eliminate the problem completely.

When Adam arrived at his office the following morning, the first thing he did was read the newspaper to find out about the reaction to his speech. This time the public reaction was positive with respect to the Chinese problem, but the general feeling was that California should never have separated from the United States in the first place. Adam was not the least bit surprised by the public reaction. Perhaps it was time to remind them that, at the time the decision was made to leave the United States, the polls indicated sixty-five percent of the population supported the plan.

Adam was having dinner with Jean that evening. When they sat down Adam commented, "I'm sure you saw the public opinion polls taken last night after my speech. I wasn't surprised, were you?"

"No, not at all. I'm sure they've forgotten about the level of support we had from the public at the time we declared our independence."

"That was my thought exactly. I would like you to find out what the level of support would be for us to make a formal request that the United States take us back."

"Would you actually do that? You were the driving force behind the call for independence, and now you want to go back to the way things were?"

"No, I don't really want to go back to the way things were before we became independent. But, once again, that decision is not mine. The people have to decide. After all, everyone, including me, makes mistakes."

"Do you now think it was a mistake?"

"Yes, I do. Hindsight is always perfect. Now I know we didn't have enough money, and we shouldn't have opened our borders to anyone who wanted to come in. We should have realized that in doing so we would create housing shortages, overcrowding at our medical facilities, an insufficient number of schools, and a lack of qualified teachers. It also exacerbated our existing drug problem. Finally, we should have known that a country the size of California cannot exist without a military."

Jean said, "I agree, we were ill prepared. But I'm not sure rejoining the United States will solve anything. All of those problems will still exist."

"No, not all. If we rejoin the United States, we wouldn't need a military force. We would be able to concentrate on resolving our other issues, but I think we would have some help from them."

"Okay, I'll try to find out how the people in the legislature feel about it."

"Thanks, Jean."

Russell Fine

XXXXII
The Oval Office
October 20, 2025

Roy knocked lightly on the door to the Oval Office. President Haskell said, "Come in, Roy."

Roy walked in and asked, "Did you see President Peterson's speech last night?

"Of course I did."

"I spoke to him an hour ago. He told me the Chinese are leaving Edwards, but they want to continue the development at 29 Palms."

"I know that. We discussed it at the meeting I had with Ambassador Collins. Apparently, and much to my surprise, the speech at the UN that California's ambassador made was very effective in mobilizing support for creating trade barriers with China."

"There are some other developments in California you are probably not aware of; President Peterson told me he asked his girlfriend, Jean Foreman, to find out how the California legislature would feel about rejoining the United States."

"I didn't realize President Peterson and Jean were close friends. I've met Jean a few times at meetings. She seems nice and very competent. I guess I'll have to start giving more thought about California rejoining the United States. Have you made progress in your analysis of how Congress feels about it?"

"I've asked at least two dozen people about it. The general feeling is that there has to be specific conditions California would have to agree to before they would consider it. The one condition everyone mentions is the elimination of their sanctuary policies. My feeling is that California would never agree to it."

"I'm not so sure. Their open border policy has caused severe strains on their finances. They might find that a requirement to close their border with Mexico gives them an excuse to do it without upsetting the people there who like the open border policy."

"My source said that if the legislature is open to the idea, they will have a vote to determine if they should request readmission to the United States."

"That sounds like a better plan than they had when they seceded from the United States. Sometime you will have to tell me who your source is."

"You really don't want to know. When this whole California mess is over, I'll tell you."

"Okay, you're right, I really don't want to know. I'll wait and be surprised."

"Did you find out anything else in your meeting I should know about?"

President Haskell thought for a few seconds and said, "There was a big shakeup in the hierarchy of the Chinese military. Apparently, the general who gave the order to create the Los Angeles quake was executed, and so were the scientists who told him exactly how to do it."

"So, I would guess the Chinese won't be doing that again anytime soon."

"Yeah, I'm sure you're right about that."

"I wonder if actions like that create positive or negative reactions among the members of the Chinese military?"

"I would think it would just make them scared, and fear is generally a negative reaction. Apparently, the general who gave the order wanted to do whatever was necessary to establish a military base in North America. He didn't care how many people were killed or how much damage was done. His plan would have worked too, if I hadn't become suspicious about the origins of the quake."

"Was anything discussed regarding the uranium facility?"

"The only comment was, 'It will not be rebuilt'."

Roy stood up and said, "Okay, I'll let you know as soon as I hear anything about the situation in California from my source." Then he left the president's office.

XXXXIII
Sacramento, California
October 22, 2025

At about 11:00 o'clock, Adam's secretary walked into his office and said, "Jean is on her way over, and she said it was very important that she see you as soon as possible".

"Okay, tell her to come in when she arrives."

Adam wondered what was so urgent. While he was thinking about that, Jean walked in. She said, "We have a problem. I did as you asked and tried to get an idea if the legislature was open to the idea of rejoining the United States. I never said it was information you wanted. In any case, the result was that a group of them are now planning a referendum to have you recalled, and they feel that despite all the problems, rejoining the United States was not a solution."

"Wow, in less the two weeks the Chinese wanted to remove me from office, and now the legislature does too. I never really wanted this job anyway. Perhaps I should resign and let some other poor bastard try doing this job."

"I don't think a majority of the people in the legislature agree with their plan, so I wouldn't worry about it. But it certainly does not look like there is sufficient support in the legislature to get them to approve rejoining the United States."

"I suspected as much. I'm a liberal, as you are, but we both know that sometimes you have to sacrifice your personal feelings in order to do what's best for the people you represent. A few weeks ago, when I accused you of being a conservative, you told me you were being pragmatic. Now, I have to be pragmatic as well. However, our colleagues in the legislature have not learned that yet. Most of them believe they know what the people need better than the people themselves. So, in this case, we'll have to let the people decide what they want, and bypass the legislature."

"What are you going to do?"

"Tomorrow evening, I'll make another televised speech. I'll tell them about our problems and potential solutions, including rejoining the United States. I'll also tell them that in two weeks we will have another referendum vote to determine which solution, if any, is preferred by a majority of our citizens."

"I suppose that's the best way to handle it. It's going to make a lot of people in the legislature upset."

"I would expect nothing less, but the will of the people supersedes the will of the legislature. If they vote in favor of asking the United States to take us back, I'll start the negotiations to make that happen. It's fortunate our constitution has a clause that permits the people to override our legislature, otherwise this would be an exercise in futility."

"Do you want any help writing your speech?"

"Thanks for the offer, but I think I can handle it. If you would like, I'll send you a copy so you can review it beforehand."

"Yes, I would appreciate that. This may be the most important speech you ever make, and it has to be right."

"I agree. I'll spend the rest of the day working on it. Please tell Ellen to set up the speech for tomorrow."

Jean replied, "I have to get back to my office because I have an appointment in twenty minutes. I'll tell her on my way out."

"Thanks."

As soon as she left, Adam began working on his speech. He realized that most people in his position would use a speech writer, but he preferred to do it all himself. He was happy to give Jean a chance to review it first.

It took him several hours to write, but when he was finished, he was pleased with what he had written. He sent a text message to Jean with the speech attached. She made a few minor changes and sent it back to him.

Ellen had arranged for his speech to be aired live at 6:15 the following evening. She also sent notices about the speech to all her media contacts.

When the information about the speech became public, several members of the legislature became incensed. They immediately realized that Adam was trying to bypass them, and they felt betrayed. Since the legislature was in session that day, members in both houses submitted resolutions condemning Adam's actions.

They also contacted the local television stations in an attempt to convince them not to broadcast the speech. All of their efforts failed.

Adam was sitting at his desk. There were several television cameras aimed at him. He felt a little nervous because he knew many of the people who would be watching weren't going to be happy with what he had to say. When he received the hand signal to begin, he said, "Good evening. As all of you know, the last several months have been very difficult for the people of California. The Los Angeles area was devastated by a manmade Earthquake, our medical facilities and our schools are now severely overcrowded, our utility costs have skyrocketed, our drug problems have increased, and the number of homeless people in California is growing every day.

"As I told you before, the quake was triggered by an explosion intentionally detonated by the Chinese for the express purpose of creating the quake that devastated Los Angeles. The death toll from that quake is rapidly approaching one thousand. I know many of you don't believe in the death penalty, regardless of the seriousness of the crime. However, the Chinese government does, and all the people who were directly responsible for causing the quake have been executed. Also, you may be interested to know that due to pressure from their trading partners, China is abandoning their military base at what was Edwards Air Force Base.

"Most of the other problems I mentioned are a result of our open border policy with Mexico. Since we declared our independence, more than one hundred fifty thousand people have crossed the border to escape the harsh realities of living in Central America. They came here hoping to find a better life, but many of them are living in shelters in conditions that are not significantly better than what they left, and many are living on the streets in our major cities. This influx of people has caused problems at our schools and our medical facilities. We have a severe shortage of bilingual teachers and school rooms. We are converting many abandoned buildings into schools, but that takes time and money. Unfortunately, we are short of both. We have added many new doctors to the staffs at our hospitals, but the average wait time in most emergency rooms exceeds two hours. That is unacceptable.

"Despite our best efforts, we have been unable to halt the flow of harmful drugs across our southern border. In Los Angeles alone, there are more than 25 deaths every week that can be directly attributed to these drugs. I don't have exact numbers for the San Francisco area, but I suspect it's similar. The Chinese ships patrolling our shoreline have put a large dent in the flow of drugs coming to California by boat, but our border is porous and there are many places to cross that are completely unguarded.

"Not all of the information I want to give you tonight is negative. We have given new oil exploration leases to all California based oil companies. They are currently doing underwater surveys to locate the places most likely to produce oil. The first exploratory wells will be started early next year. Additionally, we should have preliminary plans for the new geothermal power facility in the next sixty days. Both of those projects will help us financially, and reduce our dependence on purchased electrical power and imported oil. Also, the repairs have been completed at Diablo Canyon, and the new reactor will be online within two weeks. Then we will have sufficient power for all of you in Northern California, and you will see an immediate reduction in your electrical rates.

"Our leases with the Chinese gave a substantial boost to our treasury, so we have the money we need to continue the reconstruction in Los Angeles. Also, the Chinese have agreed to assist us in our rebuilding efforts at no cost. An obviously reasonable decision, since they were responsible for the quake. However, that money will not last very long. It's very expensive to build schools, provide free medical care, and all the other services needed by our new citizens.

"When we left the United States, we did so without fully understanding what our future needs would be. To a large extent, I feel personally responsible for that. I was so enamored with the idea of an independent California that I didn't spend enough time planning our future. In terms of population, land area, and gross domestic product, we are one of the largest countries in the world. We are also the only one without a military. We are completely unable to defend ourselves against a foreign invader. If we didn't receive assistance from the United States, and many other countries, we would all now be citizens of China. Think about the implications of that for a few moments. We may not always be able to count on assistance from other countries. Additionally, since other countries have assisted us, they could reasonably expect us to reciprocate if the need arose. We are completely unable to do that. So, if we are to remain an independent country, we need to create a military force.

"The estimates I have received indicate we would need a minimum of fifty billion dollars a year for the next five years in order to create the California military force. We simply do not have the money to do that.

"We know our tax structure hits the middle class the hardest, and the United States is aware of that as well. They are offering significant incentives to people in technical and managerial positions to relocate to the United States. So far, more than ten thousand families have accepted their offer and left California, many of them simply abandoning their homes. It won't take long before our businesses begin to experience problems caused by a lack of qualified personnel. Also, our counties are dependent on real estate taxes, and as people abandon their homes, the counties will be hurt financially as well.

"We are at a crossroads in the life of our fledgling country. The decisions we make in the next few weeks will have a substantial impact on our future. I believe we have two choices. We can remain independent, with the understanding that our taxes will very likely increase significantly, or we can ask the United States to allow us to join them again.

"The projects I mentioned earlier, and others, will produce new revenue streams. But the amount of revenue they will create is not enough to offset all of our future expenses.

"I know that becoming part of the United States again will not resolve all of our problems, but we would not have to create a military, and that's the biggest expense we will have if we remain independent.

"I will tell you now, there is extreme opposition in the legislature to any plan to rejoin the United States, and I completely understand how they feel. But in California, the people have the right to make those decisions.

"In two weeks, we will hold another referendum that will determine the future of California. I will not give you my opinion one way or the other. I want all of you to vote based on your own feelings, and think about how it affects your life. Please try not to be swayed by anything you hear from a politician.

"The government website has very specific information concerning all of the things I have talked about. I urge you to look at that information, and use it to help you make your decision. You can also send us messages with specific questions and we will try to answer them as quickly as possible.

"Thank you for your time this evening. Goodnight."

The following morning, most of the newspapers in California contained editorials calling for Adam's immediate removal from office. Every one of them called him a traitor and tool of the Washington establishment. However, many of the television stations sent reporters out to interview people on the streets and get their reactions to Adam's speech. They almost universally felt that for the first time one of their political leaders was being honest with them, and although most had not made a decision as to how they were going to vote in the upcoming referendum, they appreciated the opportunity to have a voice in California's future.

Adam had read many of the editorials, but he was not the least bit surprised. He felt somewhat depressed that none of the editorials indicated any appreciation for his candid approach to the situation. However, as he watched the live interviews on television, his depression completely disappeared. A short time later his phone rang. His assistant told him that Roy Stevens was on the phone.

He switched lines and said, "Good morning, Roy. What can I do for you?"

"I wanted you to know that both the President and I saw your speech last night. We both thought it was excellent, and should motivate your people to vote in the referendum. But you should know that there's not a lot of support in the congress for allowing California back into the union."

"I'm not surprised. I really blame myself for our current situation. If the people vote in favor of returning to the United States,

I would like to make a personal plea to a joint session of Congress. Do you think that could be arranged?"

"I'll discuss it with the President, but I don't think it'll be a problem."

"Thank you, Roy. I appreciate it. Have you seen the California newspaper editorials today?"

"Yeah, I read a few of them online. They haven't been very kind to you, to say the least."

"Yes, but apparently the people don't feel that way. I don't know how they will vote in the referendum, but they did appear to appreciate the fact that I laid out the situation honestly."

"In the end, it's the people that count, not the media. You would think that after losing three presidential elections in a row, they would realize that by now."

"Well, I didn't realize how disingenuous the media can be until the last sixty days or so. Being president of California has really opened my eyes. I'm still a liberal, and probably always will be, but now I realize that when you have to make decisions that affect millions of people, those decisions have to be based on logic, not emotions or personal preferences."

"I think that's a good thing. Not only for you, but for the people of California as well."

"Last night, before I went to bed, I was thinking about how much the democratic party has changed since John Kennedy was elected. I recently watched some old newsreel footage and I heard him say, 'Ask not what your country can do for you, ask what you can do for your country'. I wondered how many democrats still believe that way. I suspect very few."

"I'm afraid you're right. But I see things changing since the last election. The far-left wing is beginning to lose some ground, and the more moderate members of your party are gaining in power again."

"As a former member of the far-left wing, I think that's a good thing. I now realize I caused California to experiment with independence, and the experiment failed. But failure is often the best teacher, and I certainly learned a lot in the last few months."

"So, you now consider yourself a moderate democrat?"

"Yes, I guess I do."

"I'm very happy to hear that. I feel sure President Haskell will be pleased as well."

"Thank you for calling. I'll contact you as the referendum results become available."

"You're welcome. I'm anxious to know the outcome," Roy replied and he ended the conversation.

The referendum was scheduled to start on November 3, 2025 and run for five days. The results would not be announced until after the voting ended. Anyone with a valid voter ID was eligible to vote, and in case people had no access to cell phones or computers, there were computers set up in every library, post office, and police station. So, anyone who wanted to vote would be able to do so without a problem.

The referendum contained only one question:

Should California seek readmission to the United States?

Please understand there is a possibility the United States will not allow us to rejoin.

The advantage of rejoining the United States is that they will provide protection for California.

If we are not allowed to rejoin them, we will be forced to create our own military, and that would result in increased taxes.

The disadvantage is that we will be bound by the laws of the United States, and those laws are the main reason we decided to become independent.

As the date approached, almost every newspaper in California begged the people to vote 'no' in the referendum. The same was true for most of the television political pundits. However, street interviews appeared to indicate that a majority of the residents of California were in favor of rejoining the United States, and planned to vote 'yes'.

The voting started at midnight on November 3rd. By 10:00 o'clock in the morning more than five hundred thousand votes had been cast. The 'yes' votes were ahead, 54% to 46%. As Adam watched the vote tally in real time, he was pleased with the direction the vote was going, but at the same time disappointed because their attempt at independence had failed.

Late that afternoon Adam received a call from Roy. After Adam answered Roy asked, "My information indicates that the vote so far is in favor of rejoining the United States. Is that correct?"

Adam hesitated for a moment and then he said, "The status of the voting is confidential until it's completed. May I ask how you got your information?"

Roy chuckled slightly and said, "I'm sure you know we have sources inside the California government."

"Yes, I suppose so. However, I am not at liberty to either confirm or deny that your information is accurate. I promise you will be the first to know as soon as the voting is over."

"Okay, but please understand that any information I receive will only be divulged to one other person, and that's President Haskell."

"I'm sure that's true, but just as we have spies imbedded in our government, I'm positive you do as well. I don't want any information made public that could influence the vote."

"Yes, sir. I understand, and I promise that the information I have already received will remain confidential."

"Thank you, Roy. I'll call you back on the 9th, after the voting is over."

Russell Fine

XXXXIV
The Oval Office
November 6, 2025

Roy arrived a few minutes prior to his 10:00 o'clock meeting with President Haskell. Her secretary told him she wasn't in yet, but he could go inside and wait. He was surprised she had not arrived, because she was always in the office by 9:30. He waited on the sofa in the Oval office for her. By 10:10 he began to get worried, but she walked in a minute or so later. She said, "Roy, I'm sorry to keep you waiting, but I was on the phone with Prime Minister Bennet."

"What were you two talking about?"

"Bennet has only been the PM for a few weeks. He just discovered the free health care plan in England isn't working as well as everyone has been told. Last year, more than eleven hundred people died while waiting for surgery. There's a severe shortage of both doctors and nurses. He wants to work with us to set up a plan to bring patients here for surgery if the wait is potentially life threatening. I told him you would be calling him shortly."

"Okay, I can do that. Before I do, I'd like to call the administrators at several large hospitals and see how they feel about it. I assume the British government will be paying all the bills."

"I did not discuss that with him, but I'm sure they will. Anyway, the purpose of our meeting is to discuss the situation in California."

"Yes, it is. It would appear the vote will be in favor of asking to rejoin the United States. There are less than forty-eight hours left to vote, and more than seventy-five percent of eligible voters have already voted. The 'yes' votes are ahead by almost five percent."

"I suppose that's good news. I've been giving this a lot of thought, and I've discussed it with majority leaders in the House and the Senate. There's not much support for making California a state again. I haven't asked, but I think I could muster up enough votes to make California a United States territory. I think I should speak to a joint session of congress before we ask them to vote. It should be a closed session. No news coverage of any kind. I don't even want the subject of the session discussed."

"That's a good idea. I'll arrange it for tomorrow evening. I think that making California a territory is a reasonable compromise. It keeps them out of United States politics, but they will still have to obey our laws. They get the protection of the federal government, but they won't have to pay United States income taxes. I think the only problem may be immigration. They would have to close their border with Mexico."

"Yes, but President Peterson has already admitted that unfettered immigration is the primary cause of the financial situation there. So, he may be in favor of putting limits on new immigrants entering California. They have already done that to some extent, with the requirements that the people either have a job waiting or they agree to work for California."

"I discussed that recently with my contact in Sacramento. She told me that less than five percent of the people crossing the border have a job waiting for them. The other ninety-five percent are assigned to clean up and construction tasks in various parts of Los Angeles. The problem is, less than twenty-percent show up for work, half of the ones who do show up for work disappear after a week or two."

"That's a pretty abysmal situation. I'm sure those who fail to return to work still get some kind of financial assistance from the government."

"Absolutely, they get free housing, medical care, and vouchers to buy food. The bigger problem is that many of the immigrants have decided to live on the streets instead of the free government housing. They get very little in the way of assistance. There are dining areas in most of the shelters where they can go to get food, and many of the churches are providing food as well and free second hand clothing. They can get medical care at local clinics too. So, their basic needs are being met, and their overall living conditions are probably slightly better than they were in their home countries. As a result, they have almost no desire to work. I think that will change soon, because when the weather gets cold, they will be forced to seek shelter somewhere."

"Do we know how many homeless people are living in California?"

"No, not to any degree of accuracy. Before California became independent, there were about fifty thousand homeless people living there. Now, that number has at least doubled, and possibly tripled."

"I'm glad it's their problem, not ours."

Roy grimaced when he replied, "Yes, I agree. I'll arrange for your speech right after I make calls to the hospitals."

She saw the look on Roy's face and said, "I know you have a lot on your plate right now, but I also know you will do the best job possible. You always do."

"Thank you, Madam President."

The next evening at 7:00 o'clock, the Speaker of the House stood at the podium in the House chamber and introduced President Haskell. All the members of House and Senate stood up and applauded. They continued the applause until she stepped up to the podium and motioned for them to sit down. Once they were seated and the applause subsided, she began to speak.

"Distinguished members of congress, I am here tonight because I expect to receive a request from California to become part of the United States again in the near future. I realize that in the past, dealing with California has been a problem. They ignored many of our laws. Most notably, those pertaining to immigration and illicit drugs. They ignored requests from our immigration authorities to hold criminal aliens so they could be picked up by federal law enforcement agencies. Their liberal policies with regard to drugs have resulted in massive problems including a substantial increase in drug related illnesses and deaths. Their current open border with Mexico has caused the drug problem and the homeless problem to be exacerbated. Additionally, the virtually unchecked immigration is causing a serious financial hardship.

"California is in trouble. As all of you are aware, if not for the intervention of the United States and our friends, California would now be part of China. California has no military, and they could easily fall prey to almost any country with a substantial military force. We cannot allow a hostile foreign power to establish a military presence in North America.

"I have spoken to many of you about this subject over the past few weeks, and there seems to be substantial opposition to allow California to become part of the United States again. I am asking you to reconsider your position on the matter.

"In addition to a potential military threat, we could lose access to many of the technical innovations that are developed in California. These innovations are important for both our military and our personal use. Many of the largest technology companies are based in California, and we need access to their technology. Being part of the United States again would guarantee that access.

"The voting in California will be completed in a few days, and we are almost certain the people of California will vote to request readmission to the United States. I want to be prepared with an answer for them should that happen.

"I do not want the subject of this meeting to be openly discussed until after the voting is completed. That is why we barred the press from this meeting. But I urge you to discuss this among yourselves.

"Thank you for your time this evening. Goodnight, and God Bless all of you and our country."

XXXXV
Sacramento, California
November 10, 2025

When Adam arrived at his office at 7:00 o'clock, he already knew the results of the election. By a margin of about four percent, the people voted in favor of asking the Unites States to allow California to return to the union. Adam knew it was the right thing to do, but a small part of him had hoped the people would reject the idea.

His secretary was not there yet, so as soon as he sat at his desk, he called Roy. It took Roy's secretary a few minutes to locate him. A few minutes later he heard Roy say, "Good morning, President Peterson. I assume you're calling me with the results of the referendum."

"For some reason I feel positive that you already know, but I will now officially confirm that the people of California voted in favor of asking the United States to join the union again."

"Both the President and I have discussed this with congressional leaders already. There is insufficient support to allow California to rejoin the United States as a state again. They will accept California as a territory, and will consider statehood hood in ten years."

Adam was surprised by Roy's statement. After a few seconds he asked, "What, exactly, does that mean?"

Roy answered, "It means California will receive protection from the United States military, including patrolling your beaches to prevent drug smuggling. We will take back our military bases, except for 29 Palms, and the Air Force will go back to Edwards after the Chinese have vacated it. You will also receive assistance in the rebuilding of Los Angeles. However, you will be bound by all United States laws, including our immigration laws. Your border with Mexico will be closed, and immigrants who want to come here will have to file a request with our immigration department.

"As a territory, all government entities will receive financial assistance from the United States to help with the cost of running the various government agencies.

"Most of the citizens of California will not have to pay United States income tax. But all California workers will have to pay FICA and Medicare taxes. Only people who work directly for the government will be required to pay United States income tax.

"Also, as a territory, California citizens will not be permitted to vote in federal elections or have any representatives in Congress."

Adam replied, "I guess that's the price we will have to pay because of our decision to leave the United States. Am I correct that we can have our own laws as well, just as we did when we were a state?"

"Yes, so long as the laws you pass don't conflict with federal laws. I also want you to realize there will be no more sanctuary for people who cross any United States border without permission. I'm sure you know that those sanctuary laws conflict with United States laws."

"It would appear that another referendum is in order. I would like to write something that outlines what our status would be as a territory and send it to you for review. Is that okay?"

"Of course, I'll review it as quickly as possible. I've discussed this with President Haskell and she would like your response within thirty days. Is that time frame acceptable?"

"Yes, I'm sure it is. I don't know how the people will feel about no longer being a state."

"Remember, that status is temporary. In ten years, you can apply for statehood again."

"I understand. Thank you, Roy. I'll try to finish the outline that I will present to the people today. I'll call you when it's finished."

That didn't go as Adam had hoped, but he understood the situation completely. They tried to screw the United States, and now they had to pay the price. However, the more he thought about being a territory the more he liked it. There were some advantages, the first being no federal income tax. The fact that the United States would assist in rebuilding Los Angeles was also a plus, and that being part of the United States again would mean an end to them stealing California's technical and managerial workers. It would probably also mean an end to California's dependence on China. The only thing they really lose is some influence in federal politics, and based on the time he has spent as president of California, he would not miss the politics at all.

He spent several hours writing the proposition. It said:

Shall California accept the offer from the United States to become part of the United States again?

Please read the following information before voting:

In the last referendum a majority of California voters felt that rejoining the United States was the best approach to take in order to resolve California's problems. Upon completion of the voting, President Haskell's Chief of Staff, Roy Stevens, was informed of the results. We were told that President Haskell had already discussed the possibility of California becoming part of the United States again. The result of those discussions is the United States Congress would allow California to rejoin the United States, but not as a state. We would be the territory of California.

What this means is that we would have the full protection of the United States military. We will have the United States Coast Guard protecting our shoreline, instead of China. As a territory, the United States will assist us in the rebuilding of Los Angeles, and they will provide financial assistance to all government entities.

Becoming a United States territory requires that California recognize and enforce all United States laws and regulations. In essence, that means an end to our sanctuary policies. The United States government will resume control of our border with Mexico, and all law enforcement agencies in California must follow all directives received from United States Immigration authorities.

Additionally, United States Territories have no representation in Congress, and do not vote in Federal Elections.

Most of the citizens of California will not have to pay federal income tax. Only people employed by a government entity that receives funding from the United States are required to pay this tax. Everyone will be required to pay Social Security and Medicare taxes.

If we agree to become a United States territory, after 10 years, we may request to become a state again.

Please vote YES if you feel California should become part of the United States again, or NO if you feel California should remain an independent country.

Adam reread the proposition several times and then sent it to Roy for review. An hour later he received a message from Roy that the information wording of the proposition was correct. After receiving Roy's response, Adam recorded a brief speech and sent copies to all the local media outlets.

The referendum was set to begin at midnight on November 17, 2025, and would run for five days. Although information about the referendum was all over the media, the pundits were largely silent regarding it. There were only a few editorials that covered the topic, and none suggested either voting for or against rejoining the United States.

During the first full day of voting, more than sixty-five percent of eligible voters cast their ballots. The results were what Adam expected; almost seventy percent voted in favor of becoming a territory of the United States. As people were interviewed, most felt that being part of the United States again, without having to pay income tax, made the proposal acceptable. Another large group were swayed in favor of rejoining the United States because it would halt the flow of immigrants into California, and they expressed the opinion that only a very vocal, but small percentage of the California population actually favored open borders.

Adam asked his secretary to place a call to President Haskell, and fifteen minutes later he was speaking to her.

"Hello Nancy; I suppose you already know how the vote is going here, right?"

"Yes, Roy told me a few minutes ago that it is statistically impossible to change the results, so California will become part of the United States again. I believe that should happen on January 1, 2026. Would that be acceptable?"

"Yes, I think the timing is good. Sometime you're going to have to tell me who the spy in my administration is."

"You may not believe this, but I don't know. Whoever it is only speaks to Roy."

"Okay, when all this is over, I'll ask Roy."

"I'll let him know the question is coming. If it's okay with you, I'll make a formal announcement regarding California on Saturday, after the voting is completed."

"Yes, that's fine. I'll make an announcement on Saturday as well."

"I think you should be here in person when I sign the legislation making California a territory."

"That sounds like a good idea. Just let me know when. You probably know I'm a pilot, but since taking this job I haven't had much of an opportunity to fly. That trip will be a vacation."

"Okay, Adam. I'll make sure the bill is submitted next week. We'll contact you again after it's passed and set up a day and time for the signing ceremony."

"Thank you. I'm looking forward to meeting you in person."

"That goes for me too."

The next call Adam made was to Jean. He told her about his call to President Haskell, and asked her out for dinner that evening. She quickly agreed.

Adam decided to take the rest of the day off. He stopped at a jewelry store on his way home and spent a substantial amount of money. When he arrived at his house, he told his driver to take the rest of the day off.

Adam arrived at Jean's house a few minutes before 7:00 o'clock. When she opened the door, Adam hugged her, and they kissed passionately. When they separated Jean asked, "What brought that on?"

Adam stared at her and said softly, "I've been so busy these past several months that I've been forced to put my personal life on hold. Now this thing is over, I realized two things. First, while work is important, it should not be the most important thing in my life. The second is, I realized how much I love you. I don't want to live alone anymore. Will you marry me?"

Jean was silent for a few seconds. Then she smiled, put her arms around Adam and they kissed again. She whispered in his ear, "I'd love to."

Without saying another word, Adam reached into his pocket and removed the purchase he made at the jewelry store. He opened the small box, smiled, and offered it to Jean.

She looked at the ring in the box and said, "Wow, it's beautiful! I'll wear it forever." When she put ring on it was a little big. She gazed at her hand for a while and then she said, "I'll wear it forever; after we get it resized."

At dinner they talked about their wedding and decided that neither of them wanted a big affair. So, the plan was to have the ceremony in Adam's office, with Adam's friend Richard, who was also the Chief Justice of the California Supreme Court, performing the ceremony. Only a few people would be in attendance. They also agreed that the trip to Washington would serve as their honeymoon.

The following morning, when Adam arrived at his office, the first thing he did was to call Ellen and ask her to come to his office. When she walked in Adam said in a very serious tone, "I have a task for you. It's very important, but I'm sure you'll be able to handle it."

Ellen was concerned because of his tone of voice. She asked, "Is there a problem? What do you need me to do?"

Now Adam smiled and said, "I need you to arrange a wedding. Jean and I are getting married."

Now Ellen face broke into a huge grin and she said excitedly, "I'm so happy for you! It's about time. What do you want me to do?"

"We don't want anything big or elaborate. We want only a few people, and I thought we would hold it here. I would like Richard to perform the ceremony."

"I'm sure he'll be happy to do that. Do you know who you want to invite?"

"You know, I really have no friends except for you and Jean, and obviously both of you will be there. So, I think that's a question for Jean."

"Okay, do you have a date in mind?"

"You're not aware of this yet, but we will be going to Washington to witness the signing of the bill that makes California a United States territory. That will probably happen in the next two or three weeks, and we want to be married before we go."

"Okay, I'll arrange it for early next week. I'll call Richard immediately and find out when he'll be available."

"Thank you, Ellen. I really appreciate it."

"You're welcome. This is a task I will enjoy doing. Do you have any honeymoon plans?"

"Yeah, the trip to Washington. We'll be using my plane. I was thinking that maybe we would go somewhere after the signing ceremony. By the way, I haven't asked you how you feel about us becoming part of the United States again."

"I'm sure you remember that I didn't like the idea of separating from the United States in the first place. I never thought we were prepared to be our own country, and obviously I was right. So, to answer your question; I'm very happy we will be part of the United States again."

"I guess I should have listened to you when this all first started. Please let me know as soon as we have a date for the wedding, and keep Jean informed as well."

Ellen, obviously happy, replied, "My pleasure." Then she almost danced out of Adam's office.

At 1:00 o'clock Jean and Ellen walked into Adam's office. Jean walked over to Adam, kissed him lightly on his cheek, and said, "Ellen and I have finished the wedding plans."

Adam said, "That was fast. So, when will the big event occur?"

"The wedding will be held in the conference room on Tuesday, December 2nd. There will be nineteen guests, plus us, for a total of twenty-one. The big table in the conference room will be moved out and replaced with smaller tables and chairs. Richard is excited about performing the wedding. He said the last one he performed was more than twenty years ago. There will also be a photographer." Then she handed him a paper and said, "This is the guest list. Ellen has already contacted them and they all agreed to be there."

Adam quickly read the guest list and said, "This list is perfect. Did you arrange for food and drinks?"

"Yes, everything is all arranged. Since I know you can afford it, we will be serving fillets and lobster, and there will be a full bar," Ellen replied.

"That sounds perfect. I'm excited, and a little scared."

Jean asked, "Do I scare you?"

Adam laughed and said, "No, it's not you. I've never lived with anyone, other than my parents. It's going to be different having someone else around all the time."

"I promise not to get in your way."

"It's not me I'm worried about, it's you. I'm kind of a slob."

Jean smiled and replied, "I'm sure we'll get used to living together very quickly."

The next morning Adam received a call from President Haskell.

"Good morning, Nancy. How are you?"

"Very well, thank you. I hear that congratulations are in order. I met Jean several times at conferences over the years. She's a wonderful woman. I hope you two are very happy together."

"Thank you. So, you obviously have a spy here. Only the people on our guest list know about the wedding. Even the company we hired to do the catering hasn't been told the purpose of the event. I really want to know who it is."

"I already told you I didn't know, and that hasn't changed. When you're here, ask Roy.

"I will. Do you have a date for the signing?"

"Yes, the bill will be approved by congress by December 5th, and I will sign it on December 18th. Is Jean coming with you?"

"Yes, it's going to be our honeymoon. I think we'll fly to some island in the Caribbean after the signing and spend a week there."

"That sounds wonderful. Please let Roy know your schedule and we'll send a limo to pick you up. If you like, you can spend a night or two at the White House."

"Thank you, that would be wonderful."

"You're welcome. I'm looking forward to meeting you in person."

XXXXVI
Becker Aerospace
November 18, 2025

Harold Becker arrived at his office early. When he sat down at his desk, he discovered there was already a message from Roy. It said he would call at 8:30.

When the phone rang Harold said happily, "Good morning, Roy. And it's truly a good morning. In less than two months this insanity will be over and California will be part of the United States again."

"I hope you realize how important a part you and your people played in making it happen. President Haskell would like to thank you personally, and she has asked me to extend an invitation for you and your staff to come to the White House."

"Thank you, but I'm not sure that's a good idea. We could be prosecuted for the acts of insurrection we committed."

"Don't worry, that won't happen. President Haskell wouldn't allow it. In any case, nobody will really know the reason you're here. Also, at that time you will be awarded a maintenance contract from the Air Force. That will reimburse you for the expenses you incurred, and allow you to reopen your business."

"Thank you, Roy. I really appreciate it. Do you have a date for the White House event?"

"Not yet, it will be sometime in January. I'll let you know. Also, we will no longer need the scrambler for our phone calls. No one is listening. Have a wonderful holiday season Harold. I'm looking forward to meeting you and your people in person."

Russell Fine

XXXXVII
The White House
December 16, 2025

Roy and President Haskell were relaxing in the Oval Office having their morning coffee. President Haskell asked, "Have you heard from President Peterson regarding his trip here?"

"No, not since last week. I expect to hear from him again today. In our last conversation he told me that he and Jean are planning to spend two nights here. Then they are going to fly to Martinique and spend a week there before they go back to California. I've already informed housekeeping that we will have guests for the 17th and 18th. I just don't know his flight schedule."

"Since he will be flying his own plane, he can make his own schedule. Just let me know when you hear from him. Also, you should be aware that he's going to ask you who the spy is in his administration."

"Okay, it's probably not necessary to keep it secret any longer. His assistant, Ellen Miller, and I were classmates at U.C. Davis. We even dated a few times. We've stayed in touch over the years, and when California was about to declare their independence, she called me. I promised to keep our communication secret. Anyway, every time there was a new development in the California fiasco, she called me."

"Are you going to tell President Peterson when he asks?"

"Probably, but I want to make sure it's okay with Ellen. However, if President Peterson doesn't ask, I won't tell."

"That sounds very reasonable."

Three hours later Roy received a call from Adam. After exchanging greetings Adam said, "I'll be arriving at Regan at 4:00 PM tomorrow, if that's acceptable."

"That's perfect. I'm sure you will be filing a flight plan, but I'll still contact air traffic control and make sure you get priority treatment. There's a civilian terminal at Regan. I'll have a limo waiting there for you and your wife.

Due to some minor air traffic delays, Adam landed at Regan about fifteen minutes late. He taxied the plane over to the civilian terminal and followed a ground control truck to the terminal.

He stopped the plane and lowered the air stairs. As he did so a limo, with flashing lights, pulled up next to the plane. As he and Jean began walking down the stairs, a door in the limo opened and Roy Stevens stepped out.

They met at the bottom of the stairs. Roy extended his hand and said, "President Peterson, it's a pleasure to meet you sir. I'm President Haskell's Chief of Staff, Roy Stevens."

Adam replied, "First, please call me Adam. I'm a very informal person. Also, I know who you are. I've seen you on television a few hundred times. This is Jean, my wife."

Roy shook Jean's hand too and said, "It's nice to meet you as well, Jean. We'll be having dinner with President Haskell this evening, if that's okay."

Jean smiled, and replied, "Of course it's okay. It's been a few years since we last met. It will nice to see her again."

"President Haskell expressed the same feelings."

After they were all seated comfortably in the limo, Adam said, "I have a question for you, Roy. I know you have a spy in my office. Who is it?"

"I knew you were going to ask, so I asked her if it was okay to reveal her name. She said at this point it didn't really matter anymore. She is someone who attended U.C. Davis at the same time I did...."

"I'll be dammed, Ellen is the spy."

"Adam, please don't be angry with her. She was worried about the way things were going and she asked me to help."

"I'm not angry. Actually, I'm not even surprised. She didn't like the idea of an independent California in the first place, and she wasn't shy about letting me know how she felt. I'm positive she felt what she was doing was right."

Jean said, "I don't think we should tell her we know."

"I agree," Adam said. "Ellen was right, at this point it doesn't matter. I haven't lost any confidence in her, and she can continue as my assistant for as long as she wants."

The California Experiment

The dinner that evening, and the signing ceremony the following day, went exactly as planned. Since Adam was there, he formally signed the legislation indicating California's acceptance.

Russell Fine

XXXXVIII
California Territory
January, 2026

The transition to a United States Territory went very smoothly. The United States military began returning to their California bases after the bill was signed. Post office employees now worked for the United States again. The United States Border Patrol took over control of the border checkpoints at midnight. The Coast Guard also began their patrols at the same time.

President Peterson was now Governor Peterson, and an election was scheduled for the first Tuesday in March. At that time the people of California would select legislators and a new governor for the territorial government. Adam had decided not to run for governor, but Jean insisted he was the best person for the job. Other members of the legislature wanted him to run as well. So, in the end, he changed his mind.

Adam had been living in a house in Sacramento that he rented when he became president, since his home in Palo Alto was too far away. Jean liked the house, so Adam bought it, along with the entire contents.

The Chinese had abandoned Edwards, so it became Edwards Air Force Base again. In 29 Palms, the Chinese had begun construction on a large resort, and several large apartment buildings. The wells they dug were providing water, and they were nearly finished with a real sewage treatment facility.

The California Immigration Act was suspended on January 1st, but while it was active, more than sixteen thousand families took advantage of the program and left California.

Almost all of the damage caused by the Los Angeles quake had been repaired. Much of that work had been done by the Chinese. The Army Corps of Engineers was back in Los Angeles to make permanent repairs to the highways.

A large minority of the California population was very unhappy that they were now controlled by the United States again. Their leader vowed that he would do whatever was needed to make California independent again. They had already planned marches to the border to protest United States immigration policies, and other demonstrations at United States military bases. They were also planning to spend millions of dollars to elect their members to the legislature.

So, the future of California remains uncertain.

Epilog

Adam was elected in a landslide election. His two opponents were far left of Adam's more centrist positions. They wanted to close both San Onofre and Diablo Canyon, and ration electrical power until green sources of energy could be developed. They also wanted to implement new laws that would limit the use of private vehicles and ban most diesel-powered farm equipment. One of them was pushing for California to become independent again. Neither of them received more than five percent of the vote. As a result, Adam became the first governor of the California Territory since 1849.

During Adam's first term, with the help of Jean and Ellen, Adam ran California like he did his business empire. His decisions were based primarily on economics, and the result made the economy of California grow at a phenomenal pace. As his term was drawing to close, California's economy was exceeded by only the United States and China.

By the summer of 2026, the repairs in Los Angeles were completed and the freeways were opened to truck traffic again for the first time in more than a year. More than twenty new schools were either opened in existing buildings, or were under construction. There was still a shortage of bilingual teachers, but the positions were slowly being filled. In some cases, teachers who had left California when it became independent, returned.

Immediately after the United States took control of the California-Mexico border, the border fences were repaired where needed, and new border fences were erected. As a result, the people trying to come cross the border without permission came to an abrupt halt by the summer of 2026. Additionally, the flow of illicit drugs was halted as well. Plans were implemented that allowed up to five hundred people per month to enter California, but they had to apply and receive permission before they were permitted to cross the border.

However, by the end of 2028, the influx of people from Mexico and Central America who applied to become United States citizens had slowed to a point where only about three hundred people applied each month. The main reason for the decrease in new immigrants was because both the United States and California, which was now flush with cash, began to provide financial assistance to many of the Central American countries that were the primary source of new immigrants. Adam was in charge of the program, and he made sure that when assistance was given it reached the people it was intended for, not the pockets of the local politicians. He accomplished this by never providing cash. Instead, the program provided construction crews and materials to build what was needed. New roads, schools, fresh water wells, and electric power generating facilities were constructed. As a result, the living conditions in those countries were improved to the point where the residents no longer felt the need to move in order to improve their lives.

The Chinese development at 29 Palms continued to grow, and by 2030 had more than two hundred fifty thousand permanent residents. As the number of residents grew, it soon became obvious they would need to rely on California to provide essential services. Adam reached an agreement with the Chinese leadership that rescinded their "tax free" status in exchange for those services. So, the residents of 29 Palms began to pay the same taxes as all of the other California residents.

Despite Adam's success as governor, and the desire of the people that he run again, Adam decided to retire. That way he could spend more time with Jean and their daughter, Linda.

Adam's assistant, Ellen Miller, was elected governor in 2030, and she continued the policies Adam had put in place. California continued to prosper under Ellen's leadership, and when the tenth anniversary of their territorial status occurred, the people decided to remain a territory.

Made in the USA
Lexington, KY
11 November 2019